Enjoy all of these American Girl Mysteries®:

*and many more!*

— A *Molly* MYSTERY —

# CLUES IN THE SHADOWS

by Kathleen Ernst

Published by American Girl Publishing, Inc.
Copyright © 2009 by American Girl, LLC

Questions or comments? Call 1-800-845-0005, visit our
Web site at **americangirl.com**, or write to Customer Service,
American Girl, 8400 Fairway Place, Middleton, WI 53562-0497.

Printed in China
09 10 11 12 13 14 LEO 10 9 8 7 6 5 4 3 2 1

PICTURE CREDITS
The following individuals and organizations have generously
given permission to reprint illustrations contained in "Looking Back":
pp. 172–173—"Your Scrap" poster, © Swim Ink 2, LLC/Corbis;
girl holding newspapers, Library of Congress; pp. 174–175—
classroom, Library of Congress; three girls, Library of Congress;
pp. 176–177—V-E Day celebration, Corbis; soldier and girl,
National Archives; soldier with dog, Bettmann/Corbis;
pp. 178–179—Western Union, © *Seattle Post-Intelligencer* Collection;
Museum of History and Industry/Corbis; dance, Bettmann/Corbis;
"We Can Do It!" poster by J. Howard Miller/Corbis.

Illustrations by Jean-Paul Tibbles

Cataloging-in-Publication Data
available from the Library of Congress.

*For all those in my extended family who served,*
*on the home front or overseas*

# TABLE OF CONTENTS

# 1

# AN ARREST!

"Are you sure you want to go to the library *now*?" Molly asked Linda and Susan. "Before school?" The three girls stood in Linda's garage, staring at a box of books they'd collected from neighbors.

"Molly McIntire, we *must* go to the library this morning," Linda insisted. "It's our patriotic duty!"

Molly understood patriotic duty. She'd tried hard to do her part during the past three and a half years—collecting scrap metal, weeding her family's Victory garden, even learning a special tap-dance routine for the Miss Victory program. On top of all that, Molly's father was a doctor, and he had joined the Army Medical Corps when World War Two began. He'd been

1

sent to England, and although he'd been home for a month, Molly would never forget the long years her family had spent worrying that German pilots might bomb his hospital.

Her two best friends knew all that, of course. And Linda's father was still serving overseas, so Molly understood how she felt. "I just wish we could have done it yesterday evening, after our Junior Red Cross meeting," she said.

"We're not supposed to be out after dark anymore," Linda reminded her.

"I know." Molly sighed. Coal and heating oil were becoming scarce because of the war, so the government had instituted a "brownout." Business owners eliminated outdoor and display lighting. No one left porch lights on anymore. When dusk fell, the girls' familiar neighborhood became a different, slightly spooky place.

Susan was hesitating, too. "It is our patriotic duty," she said. "But we might be late for school if we go to the library now."

"We've got plenty of time," Linda scoffed. She began shoving donations into her book bag.

# An Arrest!

"And the librarian has to box up the donated books this morning. Don't you two want Jefferson to win the competition?"

"Sure," Molly said. All the public libraries in Illinois were collecting books and magazines for wounded soldiers. The library that donated the most would receive a certificate.

Molly wanted the Jefferson library to win as much as anyone. But the truth was, she just didn't get *quite* as excited about war-work contests as she used to. She didn't want to admit that, though. It wasn't patriotic.

"You're right," she said instead. "We've got time for a quick detour."

As the girls divvied up the books, a car pulled up at the curb and Linda's mother climbed out. She waved to the other women in her car pool, then trudged up the driveway. She wore grease-stained slacks and a snug-fitting blouse. A bandanna captured her hair. Molly knew how proud Linda was of her mom, who had gone to work at Jefferson's airplane factory to help the war effort.

"Good morning, girls," Mrs. Rinaldi said. She kissed her daughter on the top of her head. "Did you get breakfast, Linda?"

"Yes, and I packed lunches for Joey and me, too." Joey was Linda's younger brother.

"Thanks." Mrs. Rinaldi managed a tired smile, and turned to Molly and Susan. "Did Linda tell you that I got switched to third shift? I'm still getting used to working all night and sleeping during the day."

Molly didn't like the long hours her own mother worked at the Red Cross office, but at least her mother didn't have to be away over-night! Thankfully, kind neighbors took turns staying at the Rinaldi house, so Linda and Joey weren't alone. Molly sometimes thought that the war had brought out the best in many people— people who were quick to help out wherever they were needed.

"What you're doing must be very important," Susan said.

"Yes, but I can't tell you any more about it." Linda's mother made a quick gesture in front of her mouth, like turning a key. "Loose lips can sink ships, you know. Now, you girls have a good day at school."

The girls headed out with their heavy book bags thumping against them. April had just turned to May. Pools of yellow daffodils and purple crocuses bloomed in gardens. Cardinals and robins sang their springtime songs. The warm sunshine seemed full of hope. *Maybe we won't be late for school*, Molly thought. Maybe Dad wouldn't have to work so hard at the veterans' hospital, and Mom wouldn't have to work so hard for the Red Cross. Maybe the war really would be *over* soon. Molly wanted that more than anything.

Then Molly saw Ronnie Vanko coming toward them, and her bubble of hope popped. Last year, Ronnie and his mother had moved into the little house right behind Molly's and next door to Linda's. He was a skinny boy with dark eyes that always seemed to be half shut, either in an angry squint or in a lazy "who cares" sort of way. Ronnie's two pleasures seemed to be bragging about his father, who was in the air force, and tormenting the girls in his class—Molly, Linda, and Susan included.

"You dumb girls are going the wrong way!" he hooted now.

"We are not!" Linda retorted. "We're going to—"

"Oh, come *on!*" Molly interrupted. They would definitely be late if they stopped to argue with stupid Ronnie Vanko!

The girls reached the library just as Mrs. Baker was unlocking the front door. "Gracious!" the librarian said, surveying the panting trio. "Are you playing hooky today?" The library was on Main Street, in the center of town near the post office, the town hall, and shops and businesses—but several blocks from the elementary school.

"Oh, no," Susan assured her. "We brought books to donate!"

"We were going to come yesterday evening, but we ran out of time before the brownout started," Molly explained.

"I'm glad you didn't try to come after dark," Mrs. Baker told them. "I'll be glad when we can leave safety lights on again."

"We're not too late, though, are we?" Linda asked anxiously.

Mrs. Baker smiled. "You made it in the nick of time! Here, I'll take those books. Quickly, now. You girls need to scoot to school!"

Molly grinned at her friends. "I'll race you!" She bolted down the library steps and took off.

"No fair, Molly!" Susan called. "You got a head start!"

Molly could hear the *slap-slap* of her friends' shoes against the sidewalk right behind her, and she managed an extra burst of speed. Just when she'd pulled ahead, though, a siren split the morning.

The girls skidded to a halt as a police car turned a corner onto Main Street. The car pulled over and parked in front of the telephone company building just ahead of them. Two police officers jumped from the car and hurried into the building.

"There's been some kind of trouble!" Susan gasped. "We should get out of here!"

"Hold on," Linda objected. "I want to see what happens!"

Molly hesitated, feeling some of both Susan's nervousness and Linda's curiosity. Before the girls could move, the front door of the telephone company opened again. The two policemen emerged with a third man held firmly between them. The man in the middle was tall and thin. He wore a blue and brown plaid jacket. His close-cropped hair was startlingly red—almost orange, really. None of those details fit Molly's image of a robber or gangster.

Then she caught a glimpse of the man's face. He looked mad at the world. As the policemen marched him to the curb, the red-haired man tried to pull from their grasp.

"Cut that out, Fletcher!" one of the police officers barked. "You slugged somebody, so now you're going to jail. Simple as that."

Fletcher tried again to break free. "I might as well have bought the farm, for all that anybody—"

"Save it for the judge!" the second officer said. The officers shoved Fletcher into the police car's backseat, slammed the door, and got in the front. A moment later the car disappeared down the street.

"Gosh," Linda breathed. "I've never seen anyone get arrested before."

Molly crossed her arms over her chest, suddenly feeling cold. She wished she hadn't gotten such a good look at the man called Fletcher.

# 2
# A CHALLENGE

Molly, Linda, and Susan *were* late for school. They told Mrs. Crenshaw, their teacher, about the Victory Book Campaign. Linda did most of the talking, and she used the phrase "patriotic duty" three times.

"Next time, please, don't be late for class," Mrs. Crenshaw said sternly. "Take your seats, girls."

"Yes, ma'am," they chorused. Molly was relieved that they'd gotten off so lightly.

As the day passed, Molly found herself struggling to concentrate. The big classroom windows were open, and the sharp scent of new-cut grass mixed with the musty smell of chalk dust. Every so often an image of the man in the plaid jacket popped into her mind. It was hard to focus on geography and grammar when she'd seen a man arrested! Why had he punched someone? What did buying a farm have to do with the telephone company?

The last subject of the afternoon was arithmetic, Molly's least favorite. Molly hoped Mrs. Crenshaw wouldn't call on her today. She felt too fidgety to wrestle numbers into their proper places.

"Boys and girls, clear your desks," Mrs. Crenshaw called, surprising them. "We have a special visitor this afternoon. Please welcome Miss Darleen Delaney, a Red Cross volunteer."

Molly and her two best friends exchanged delighted grins as their guest entered the room. Miss Delaney was as pretty as a movie star, with blonde hair curled in the latest style. And although she had graduated from high school two years ago, the girls considered her a friend.

"Good afternoon," Miss Delaney said. Her voice was naturally quiet, so the children who were rustling or scuffing their feet had to settle down. "It's nice to meet you. Of course, I already know some of you from our Junior Red Cross meetings."

Molly beamed. She, Linda, and Susan had joined the JRC earlier that year. And of all the people who had helped the JRC girls, Miss Delaney was their favorite. She encouraged them, even if the blankets they knitted for wounded soldiers came out a little crooked, or if they didn't collect as much money as they had hoped during war-bond drives. And if someone was especially worried about a father or brother off fighting in the war, Miss Delaney always had time to listen. She didn't make fake, cheery promises as some adults did when talking to kids. Somehow, though, everyone felt better after talking with Miss Delaney.

Molly sat up straight, her hands neatly folded on her desk. Then she noticed that Ronnie Vanko, who sat next to her, was—as usual— slouched in his seat. "Sit up!" she hissed at him. Ronnie made a face, but he did sit up a little straighter.

"I'm here to announce a very important new project," Miss Delaney began. "It's called the Paper Trooper Campaign."

Molly suddenly wanted to slump in her seat just like Ronnie Vanko.

Howie Munson began waving his arm frantically. Miss Delaney nodded in his direction. "Yes?"

"Do you mean a waste paper drive?" Howie asked.

"That's right," Miss Delaney told him. "The paper will be used by the military."

"We had a big paper drive when we were in third grade," Howie said, looking pleased with himself. "We collected so much that the army couldn't even use it all."

"There *was* a surplus of paper for a while," Miss Delaney agreed. "But it's gone now, and the army needs your help again."

Molly's hand shot into the air so fast that when Miss Delaney called on her, it took her a few seconds to realize what she wanted to say. She stood politely beside her chair. "But

Miss Delaney, my dad says the Germans are going to surrender any day now."

"I pray that's true," Miss Delaney said softly. "But remember, we're also at war with Japan. Our brave soldiers face fierce fighting in the Pacific Islands."

Molly slipped back into her seat, feeling heat flush her cheeks. She knew that, of course! But she was so used to worrying *most* about what was happening across the Atlantic Ocean, where her father had been stationed, that she sometimes had no worry left for what was happening in the Pacific.

"This is a time to rededicate ourselves to the war effort," Miss Delaney told them. "The armed forces need paper for wrapping rations, for making shell and cartridge boxes, for putting protective bands on bombs, and for many other things." She opened her arms, as if to make sure that every child felt included. "We need your help."

Molly looked down at her hands. It sometimes felt as if the war would *never* end. The fighting had been dragging on for so long that she could hardly remember what life was like without big black clouds of war hanging over their heads.

Miss Delaney eyed the silent classroom with a knowing little smile. "Some of you may be thinking that paper drives aren't very exciting. General Eisenhower thought that might be the case. That's why he came up with a special plan."

General *Eisenhower?* He was one of America's smartest and bravest generals. Molly glanced at Linda and Susan. They both raised their eyebrows, looking impressed. Even Ronnie was paying close attention.

"General Eisenhower knows how hard the children of this country have been working to end the war," Miss Delaney was saying. "So he decided that those who work the hardest deserve medals."

Molly felt her own eyebrows shoot up toward her bangs. Medals? From General Eisenhower? For *kids?*

A big map of Europe was hanging over part of the blackboard. Mrs. Crenshaw gave the map a quick jerk. It rolled up neatly on its rod, revealing a poster. Even from the middle of the room, Molly could see the image of a gold medal hanging from a red and white ribbon. The medal showed the head and shoulders of General Eisenhower himself.

"Wow," Howie said, forgetting to raise his hand. "I'd sure like to get one of those."

"Perhaps you can," Miss Delaney told him. "A General Eisenhower Waste Paper Medal will be awarded to every student who collects a thousand pounds of waste paper by the end of next month."

A burst of chatter rippled through the room—half excited, half dismayed. Molly didn't know what to think.

"Children who aren't able to reach that goal may still earn a Paper Trooper Distinguished Service certificate," Miss Delaney added. "The Red Cross will present the awards at a special reception at the end of June. Mrs. Crenshaw will tell you when and where to deliver the paper you collect. Good luck!"

"Are you going to try to earn a medal?" Susan asked her friends later that afternoon. They had just been dismissed from school.

Molly considered as they went down the steps to the sidewalk. "I don't know," she said slowly. "A thousand pounds is a lot of waste paper!"

"A thousand pounds is a lot of waste paper!" a high, mocking voice repeated behind her.

Molly whirled to face Ronnie Vanko. "Shut your trap, Ronnie!"

"Aw, try and make me," Ronnie said. "You're just dumb girls. You couldn't earn that medal if you tried."

Linda glared at him. "We could so! You're the one who couldn't win it. You never help out with *anything*. When the boys gathered tinfoil to be made into tanks and trucks, you hardly did any work."

Ronnie scowled. "That was a stupid project. Just like it's stupid to give kids medals for collecting paper. Medals are for *real* heroes, like my dad. He's still in the war, and he's earned lots of medals. *My* dad would never leave the fighting early like—"

"My dad's a hero too!" Molly yelled.

"That's right," Linda declared. "It's not as if Dr. McIntire ran away from the war or something. The army *sent* him home so he could help wounded soldiers—"

"Far away from any danger," Ronnie interrupted.

Molly's hands curled into fists. "You just shut up!" she began. "You don't know—"

"Children!" a woman's voice snapped. "Stop fighting at once."

Molly looked up and saw Mrs. Hargate glaring at them. Her daughter, Alison, who was in their class, stood behind her mother. Mrs. Hargate often came to walk Alison home from school.

"You should be ashamed of yourselves,"

# A CHALLENGE

Mrs. Hargate went on. "Come along, Alison." Mrs. Hargate walked away, her heels making little clicking noises on the sidewalk. Alison's mother always looked as if she were on her way to a cocktail party.

Ronnie stomped off in the other direction. The girls stared after him. "I wish Ronnie Vanko had never moved to Jefferson," Molly grumbled. She kicked a rock from the pavement.

"Me too," Linda said. "I don't know why Ronnie even bothers coming to school. He doesn't do his homework half the time."

"He hasn't tried to make friends, either," Molly added. During recess Ronnie usually stood in a corner of the playground by himself, hands in his pockets. Just that day, Molly had heard Woody Halsey ask Ronnie if he wanted to play ball with the other boys. Ronnie had just shaken his head.

"Forget Ronnie," Susan said. "Come on. Let's go."

Molly followed her friends down the school steps. She wasn't ready to forget what Ronnie had said, though. *I'll show him*, she thought. One way or another, she was going to put Ronnie Vanko in his place!

# 3
# RICKY THE RAT

Molly smelled something warm and spicy
when she opened her front door that afternoon.
She started for the kitchen but stopped short.
"Dad!" she cried happily. "What are you doing
home so early?" Dr. McIntire was sitting in his
favorite old plaid chair, reading the newspaper.
Molly's younger brother, Brad, was lying on
the living room floor, playing with some model
airplanes.

"I'm working a split shift today," Dad said.
"Got a hug for me?"

Molly dropped her book bag on the floor.
The next thing she knew she was being squeezed
into her father's arms. When Dad laid his cheek
on the top of Molly's head, she closed her eyes
and squeezed him back. She could smell the faint

tang of the aftershave he used, and the lingering vanilla aroma of his pipe. His arms felt warm and solid. Molly knew she'd never catch up on Dad's hugs.

Finally he let her go. Molly perched on the arm of his chair. "Does a split shift mean you have to go back to the hospital again?" she asked.

"I'm afraid so." His brown eyes crinkled a little at the corners as he regarded her. "So. Tell me about your day."

Molly felt a ripple of sadness. Before the war, Dad would never have said, "So. Tell me about your day." He would have boomed, "Gosh and golly, olly Molly, what have *you* done today?" But before Dad came back from England, Mom had warned her that war leaves scars on people—"and not just the kind you can see," she'd added. Molly worried a lot about Dad's scars.

Then she looked at Dad. His eyes were still warm and his arms still strong enough to give hugs. He still loved her. That was all that really mattered—and besides, now that he was home, he'd surely start to forget about the bad times in England. He'd surely start to laugh again.

So Molly told him about the Paper Trooper Campaign. "And every student who collects a thousand pounds of waste paper will win a real medal from General Eisenhower," she concluded.

"That sounds like quite an honor," Dad said. "You don't look too excited, though."

"It's just that—"

*"Vroom!"* Brad's voice rose as he swooped one of the airplanes above his head. He made a whistling noise, then dropped a little ball of crumpled paper as if it were a bomb falling from the plane. "Ker-*pow!*"

"Dad, let's go into the other room," Molly said. She grabbed his hand and towed him into the kitchen.

Mrs. Gilford, their housekeeper, was already getting out plates for an afternoon snack. "I wish I could serve you chocolate cake, Dr. McIntire," she said. "But I'm afraid this Boston Brown Bread will have to do."

"Now that the war in Europe is just about over, maybe food won't be rationed so much," Molly said hopefully.

Mrs. Gilford shook her head. "Our sugar ration is being cut again, and I can't buy any meat but scraps as it is."

Molly rested her chin on her hand. "But *why*?" It didn't seem fair.

"There are millions of hungry people in Europe who have lost their homes and farms because of the war," Dad told her. "America needs to share food with them."

"We can tighten our belts," Mrs. Gilford said. "But I'd like to give a piece of my mind to anyone who hoards rationed supplies, or buys them on the black market. Why, the grocer told me that just this morning someone tried to buy sugar with counterfeit ration coupons!"

Molly knew about the black market, the term used for the illegal sales of rationed goods, because she'd once stumbled onto some men stealing sugar from the Red Cross. "It's hard to believe people could be so selfish," she said.

"Most people aren't," Dad said.

Molly heard another *ker-pow!* from the living room. "Excuse me," she said.

Brad was still pretending to make bombing raids with the model planes. "Brad, stop it!" Molly hissed, crouching beside him. "You'd be in trouble if Mom was home to hear you! How many times has she told us that Dad needs peace and quiet?"

Brad's face puckered. "I was just playing!"

Molly sighed. Brad was only six. He didn't even remember the old cheerful, teasing Dad. "We need to do what Mom says," she told her brother. "Besides, aren't those some of Ricky's model planes? He'll be mad too if he catches you playing with them." Their brother Ricky was thirteen, and he knew how to drive them crazy.

"Can I take Bennett out to play?" Brad asked.

"Sure," she told him. "But whatever you do, don't make too much noise!" She waited until Brad whistled for the dog and they disappeared outside.

Back in the kitchen, Dad was still seated at the table. "So, Molly. Are you going to try to earn one of those Eisenhower medals?"

"I guess so." Molly took a bite of bread.

Dad reached across the table and put his hand over Molly's. "What's troubling you?"

"You know Ronnie Vanko, who lives behind us now? Well, Ronnie said—" She stopped abruptly. She couldn't repeat Ronnie's nasty comments. Ronnie had practically called Dad a coward!

"You know," Dad said, "it often helps to talk about your problems."

Molly struggled to find the right words. "Mostly he just brags a lot about his dad, the big war hero," she said finally. "And Ronnie said he didn't think I could win one of those medals."

"He must not know you very well, then," Dad said.

Molly looked at her father. His trim uniform made him more handsome than ever. Dashing, even. "Dad," she said. "What was it like for you in England?"

He looked startled. "Well...it was difficult. All of the doctors and nurses worked very hard."

"Did you get scared?"

Dad got up and fetched Mom's old knitting bag from the counter. Molly watched as he pulled out needles and yellow yarn and began to work on the scarf he was knitting. It still felt strange to see her father knitting. He'd come home with the habit. "One of the nurses taught me," he'd said. "It keeps my fingers nimble for surgery."

Now Dad knit several stitches before replying. "Yes, Molly. Sometimes I got scared."

"Did your hospital ever get bombed?"

"There were times when..." Dad's voice trailed away.

Molly remembered the advice he had just given her. "Sometimes it helps to talk," she said.

Dad smiled again, but this time it didn't seem to reach his eyes. "You're right, Molly. But I don't think that this is one of those times."

Molly looked at her plate. She could be a good listener! Didn't Dad realize how much she'd matured while he was away?

Then Ricky burst into the kitchen, followed by Molly's big sister, Jill. "Hi, Dad!" Ricky said. Jill, who was the oldest, kissed Dad's cheek.

"Molly was just telling me about the Paper Trooper Campaign," Dad told Ricky and Jill. "Are you two going to participate?"

"I'm working on a costume jewelry drive for the Red Cross," Jill reminded them. "Mom says the soldiers fighting in the Pacific islands have a much easier time when they meet the native people if they can present a pin or bracelet as a sign of goodwill. With my volunteer work at the veterans' hospital, I've got all I can handle already."

"The JRC girls are going to visit the veterans' hospital next week," Molly said. "We're making friendship bags for the soldiers."

"That will be nice," Jill said. "The patients appreciate even the littlest thing."

Molly frowned. She didn't like hearing the JRC project described as "the littlest thing."

"That's a wonderful thing to do, Molly," Dad

added. Then he turned to Ricky. "How about you? Are you going after an Eisenhower medal?"

"Yeah," Ricky said, grabbing a piece of bread. "I'll have to scramble, though. I've got a full schedule, too." As a trained plane spotter, Ricky spent several hours each week making sure that none of the planes passing overhead belonged to the enemy. He had also volunteered to mow lawns, dig gardens, and do other chores for neighborhood women who needed help.

"I'm proud of you, son," Dad said.

Molly shot a look at her brother. Ricky didn't need to sound so noble! He'd done his share of complaining about chores while Dad was away. Molly almost said so, too. Then she remembered what Mom had told her children over and over: No bickering now that Dad's home.

As Molly finished her bread, she thought about the paper drive. Maybe she *should* try to win an Eisenhower medal. Maybe that would make Dad grin at her and boom, "Gosh and golly, olly Molly, that is surely the most wondrous accomplishment imaginable!" Maybe that would help him realize that just like Jill and Ricky, Molly had done some growing up while he was away, too.

The next day was Saturday. Linda and Susan had agreed to meet at Molly's house that morning. They sat in the backyard swing, watching Ricky shoot baskets. The McIntires' swing was just wide enough for all three of them, if they squeezed together. They'd been swinging and giggling and sharing secrets in the backyard every summer that Molly could remember.

"I've decided that I really want to win an Eisenhower medal," she announced.

"You do?" Susan asked.

"I do," Molly said firmly.

Susan gave her a sideways look. "You want to show up Ronnie Vanko, don't you."

"Well, partly," Molly admitted. *And partly I want to prove to my dad that I can do it*, she added silently.

Linda gave the swing a good push with her feet. "You can have my family's paper," she said. "I've got to watch Joey so often that I wouldn't be able to win a medal anyway."

"My mom said I can't start another project until my history grade goes up," Susan added. "You can have the paper from our house, too."

"Gee, thanks!" Molly grinned at her friends. "That will help a lot!"

"We need a plan," Linda began. "We can help you collect— Oh, look!"

When Molly looked where Linda was pointing, she saw Ronnie Vanko pulling a red wagon down his driveway toward the street. He turned onto the sidewalk and was quickly lost from sight.

"He must be collecting paper too!" Molly fumed. "He never bothered to help with war projects before."

"He probably wants an Eisenhower medal so he can brag about it," Susan said.

Molly didn't think she could stand it if Ronnie won a medal and she didn't. "Let's go see if the

neighbors have any paper," she said, jumping
to her feet. "Wait here. I'll tell Mom we're heading out."

As Molly headed inside, Mom appeared at
the back door, wearing her Red Cross uniform.
"Ricky," she called. "It's almost nine o'clock.
Don't forget you promised to weed Mrs. Petroski's
garden this morning."

"Do you have to work today, Mom?" Molly
asked as she followed her mother inside. "It's
Saturday!"

"I know," Mom said. She sat down at the
table beside an almost-empty cup of coffee and
a rumpled edition of the morning paper. "But
I have to visit a young mother across town.
The army has declared her husband Missing
in Action."

"Oh no," Molly said slowly. "That's so sad!"

"It's worse than you may realize," Mom said.
"Many families have a hard time financially if
their soldier is declared missing. I'm hopeful that
the Red Cross can help the young mom out."

When Molly thought about all the good

things the Red Cross did, she understood why Mom worked so hard. Still... "I wish you could stay home more," Molly said. She slid into the chair beside her mother.

"I do too," Mom said softly. "But when I get tired or frustrated, I remind myself how lucky our family is. After all, Dad came home to us, safe and sound."

Molly looked up at her mother. "Do you really think Dad's okay?" she asked. "Since he got home he seems... different."

Mom looked thoughtful. Molly loved the way her mother always took her questions seriously. "Well, you're right," Mom agreed. "He's still adjusting to being home. He's dealing with memories from his time in England. Bad memories."

"Do you think he'll get back to normal?" Molly asked anxiously.

"I think Dad will be just fine. We need to be patient, and careful not to add to his burdens." Mom smoothed the collar on Molly's shirt, then leaned close and kissed her cheek. "Now, I really must be off. What are your plans for the morning?"

"Susan and Linda and I are collecting for the paper drive."

"Wonderful!" Mom said. "You know, Brad's old baby buggy is in the attic. That might work well to haul what you collect."

"That's a great idea!" Molly grinned. "And are you finished with the morning newspaper?"

Ricky banged in the back door as she spoke. "Hey, no fair," he complained. "I'm collecting paper too, and I was going to take it!"

"Too bad and so sad," Molly said. "I asked first."

"But—"

"*Hush!*" Mom's voice was stern. "You children must not squabble! What if your father were home to hear you? As far as I'm concerned, you can divide our scrap paper in half."

"Sorry, Mom," Molly said. She gave her brother a sour look.

"You can have the newspaper," Ricky told her. "I'll be getting *lots* from other places." He left the room with a jaunty whistle.

Molly's eyes narrowed. It wasn't like Ricky to give in so quickly. Was he up to something?

Linda and Susan helped Molly haul the old baby buggy down from the attic, and the girls set out. Mrs. Petroski, the widow who lived next door, waved from her porch. "Yoo-hoo!" she called. "I've got a few cookies left!"

The girls didn't need a second invitation. Mrs. Petroski didn't have any children, but she liked to call herself "the neighborhood grandma." She saved her sugar allowance to bake ginger-snaps for visitors. When her cat, Marmalade, had babies, Mrs. Petroski let all the kids crawl into her closet to see the kittens. And she never, *ever* complained if someone hit a ball into her begonias.

Molly told her she was collecting paper. "Oh, I've already had several children ask for my paper," Mrs. Petroski said. A faint accent hinted at her European birth, but her English was perfect. "And I can't play favorites. When I have scrap paper, I'll put it out on my front step. Finders keepers, as they say!"

"That's fair," Molly agreed.

Mrs. Petroski winked. "You're a clever girl, Molly McIntire," she said. "I have a feeling you'll earn that medal." The widow's encouragement did even more for Molly's spirits than the gingersnaps.

By the end of the afternoon, the girls had filled the baby carriage several times. When Linda and Susan helped Molly trundle the last load back home, they saw that Ricky had started a paper pile in the garage.

"You shouldn't store your paper in here too," Linda warned Molly. "It would be too easy for your piles to get mixed up with his."

Molly nodded. "Let's put mine in the garden shed," she said.

After hauling the last scrap to the little shed in the backyard, Molly surveyed her piles with satisfaction. She had a long way to go, but she was on her way to earning one of those gold medals.

Linda and Susan spent Sunday with their families. After lunch Molly set out on her own. All the businesses downtown were closed, but several shop owners had promised to leave paper by their back doors.

She was tired by the time she had gathered everything and pushed the load back to her yard. Struggling to keep even the smallest scrap from dancing away in the breeze, she gathered an armload of paper and pushed the shed door open with her hip.

Then she stopped. Her tidy piles of paper were spilling over. Some of the newspapers had been tossed on the floor. Someone had been in here—messing with her paper!

"Ricky," she muttered angrily. "That rat!"

# 4
## THE PROWLER

Molly stared grimly. Was some of her hard-earned stash gone? Now that the stacks had been disturbed, she couldn't even tell.

She turned around, ready to storm out and look for her brother, when another thought flickered through her mind. The garden shed was close to Ronnie Vanko's yard. Was Ronnie trying to take the easy way out by helping himself to some of her paper?

Still fuming, Molly tidied up her stacks and added the new donations. Then she grabbed the thick pencil Mrs. Gilford used to mark seed envelopes. Molly wrote DO NOT TOUCH in big block letters on a piece of plain paper, put it on top of the stack nearest the door, and anchored it in place with garden shears. If Ricky or Ronnie tried to steal paper again, at least they'd know she was suspicious.

That evening, after Dad had gone to work at the hospital and Brad had gone to bed, Molly, Ricky, Jill, and Mom gathered around the kitchen table. Mom paid bills while the others finished their homework. Bennett snored in his bed in the corner, twitching happily with doggie dreams.

When Molly completed her spelling, she slid her papers back into her book bag. "All done," she announced. "Mom, do you have any more scrap paper?"

Mom nodded. "I put a few old catalogs in the living room."

"You can have them all, Molly," Ricky said. His voice was sweet as honey—the tone he used when he was trying to make adults think he was a perfect son and brother.

Molly shot him a look that meant *I'm watching you, Ricky McIntire!* Then she said just as sweetly, "Thank you, Ricky."

Molly found the catalogs by the front door. She didn't want to wait until morning to take them out to the shed. She could just hear Ricky saying, *Why, since you didn't take them right away, I figured you didn't want them!*

She opened the front door and went outside. The sun had set, and because of the brownout, the yard was full of shadows. Molly hurried around the house. Staying as close as she could to the spill of light from the kitchen window, she carefully skirted the Victory garden and several clumps of tulips.

Suddenly a shadow separated from the deeper black of the shed. A *man's* shadow. A startled scream tore from Molly's throat.

The man ran. A branch snapped as he crashed through the lilac bushes at the back of their yard.

The back door to Molly's house banged open. "Molly?" Mom cried. "Is that you?" She switched the outside light on. Jill was right behind her. Bennett darted past them both, barking frantically.

# THE PROWLER

Molly ran gratefully toward the yellow glow. "I saw a prowler!" she gasped. "A man was by the garden shed!"

Mom put an arm around Molly's shoulders. "Are you sure?"

"Yes, Mom! I'm sure!" Molly replayed that startled moment in her mind. The man had been very tall, and so close that she'd caught a whiff of cigarette smoke before he dashed away.

"I wish Dad were home," Jill said.

"Come inside," Mom ordered. "I'm calling the police."

"I know what I saw," Molly insisted an hour later.

"I'm sure you do," said Officer Steves patiently. "But there's nothing to see now."

They were standing by the back steps. Molly had waited there with Mom, Jill, and Ricky while the policeman strode back and forth in the yard, shining a strong flashlight beam in front of him.

The policeman was polite, but he made Molly feel as if he thought she'd imagined the prowler. When Bennett whimpered anxiously, she scooped him up and buried her face in his fur for a moment. At least her dog believed her! "I saw him," she said again. "And I heard a branch break when he ran away."

"There is a small branch on the ground," Officer Steves said. "But it could have been broken by a squirrel."

"Didn't the guy leave any footprints?" Ricky asked.

Officer Steves shrugged. "We haven't had rain in two weeks, son. The ground's too firm for anything like that." He looked at Mom. "I'm sorry, ma'am. There's nothing more I can do."

"I understand," Mom said. "I'm sorry we called you out for nothing."

"No, no, you shouldn't feel bad," the officer assured her. "Lots of people are feeling jumpy because of the brownout."

*But I wasn't feeling jumpy!* Molly thought stubbornly.

Officer Steves added, "Since the brownout started, some citizens have formed neighborhood watches."

"We could do that!" Ricky said eagerly.

"Now, don't try to *catch* a prowler," the policeman said sternly. "But if you do see a prowler, note the time and where he goes. If the moon is out, you might even be able to see what he's wearing. Then call us. We're short-staffed because of the war, but we'll send somebody over if we can."

*If we can?* Molly thought. That statement didn't provide much assurance!

"And you can always turn a porch light on," the policeman was saying. "Or make some noise. That'll scare away just about anyone."

Mom thanked him before herding her three oldest children back into the kitchen. "Well, that was a bit of unexpected excitement," she said with a weak smile. Then the smile faded, and she regarded them seriously. "Brad is sound asleep, but I need to ask you a favor. I . . . I don't think we should mention this to Dad."

Molly blinked. "Not tell Dad?"

"Why not?" Ricky asked.

"Because she doesn't want to upset him, of course," Jill said.

"I would never ask you to lie to your father," Mom said quickly. "I just don't want to give him something new to worry about."

"Anyway, it was probably just some neighbor taking a shortcut," Jill said.

"Then why did he run away?" Molly demanded.

"Well, you screamed like a hyena," Ricky said. "The guy was probably more scared of you than you were of him. And then he was too embarrassed to come back and show his face."

"Bennett went crazy," Molly reminded him.

Ricky shook his head. "Yeah, but only *after* you screamed."

Mom leaned against the counter. "So, are we agreed?"

"Of course," Jill said, and Ricky added, "Sure, Mom."

Molly bit her lip. It didn't feel good to keep a secret from Dad. And she wasn't convinced that the man she'd seen was a neighbor. For some reason she thought again of Fletcher, the man in the plaid jacket, and a little shiver iced over her skin. *He's in jail,* she told herself firmly. Besides, it was ridiculous to think—

"Molly?" Mom asked. "Are we agreed?"

"Oh—sure," Molly echoed. But she didn't like what had happened that evening. Not one bit.

"I'll keep watch tonight," Ricky said enthusiastically. "I can sit on the back steps."

Mom shook her head. "I appreciate your offer, Ricky, but no," she said. "Your activities don't leave much time for homework as it is. Let's try to forget all about it now."

Molly knew better than to protest. But how could she forget about what had happened? *She'd* been the one startled by the prowler. She was the one who knew he was real.

"The man was by your garden shed?" Susan squealed.

"Right beside it," Molly confirmed. The girls were walking to school on Monday morning.

"That's spooky," Linda said. "Do you think it was a burglar?"

"I hope not." Molly watched a robin with a twig in its mouth fly into a bush. The air smelled like violets. Signs of spring were everywhere, but Molly's spirits felt wintry.

"Well…" Susan considered. "The prisoner-of-war camp isn't too far from Jefferson. Maybe one of the enemy soldiers escaped and was trying to sneak through your yard!"

Molly stared at her. She knew that some captured German prisoners were being held in Illinois, but it had never occurred to her that one might escape!

But Linda shook her head. "No, that doesn't make sense. Why would an escaped prisoner be in Molly's backyard?"

"You're right," Molly chimed in quickly. "If a prisoner *had* escaped, the police would have been hunting for him. The officer who came to my house just said the brownout was making everyone jumpy."

"Well, at least you scared the guy off," Linda said.

Molly hitched up her book bag's strap more securely on her shoulder. "I've got another problem, too. I took some paper into the garden shed yesterday afternoon, and I could tell that someone had been inside."

"Oh my gosh!" Susan exclaimed. "Did you tell the policeman?"

The girls reached a corner, and Molly checked for traffic before stepping into the street. "No," she said. "I don't know if anything was taken from the shed yesterday. All I know for sure is that someone messed up the paper I'd been collecting. My two suspects are Ricky and Ronnie."

"So, what are you going to do?" Linda asked. "We can't let those two ruin your chances for earning a medal!"

Molly glanced over her shoulder to make sure no one was within earshot. "For starters,

I'm going to keep a closer eye on the shed. Maybe I can catch Ronnie or Ricky trying to steal some of my paper."

Susan's eyes narrowed with satisfaction as she imagined that scene. "It would be great to catch one of them red-handed!"

"Yes, it would!" Molly agreed. "And I might even spot the prowler. The policeman suggested that we keep watch in the evenings. Mom's too tired to do it, and she told Ricky that he couldn't, either. But I can sit on the back steps for a while at night. If someone comes, I'll try to get a better look at him. And if I feel scared, I can just jump back inside and call for help." She looked from Linda to Susan. "And I hope you both will be willing to do that at your houses, too. We can start tonight, after the JRC meeting."

"Ooh!" Linda looked excited. "We can be detectives—just like Nancy Drew!"

"I don't know," Susan said, hunching her shoulders. "We don't know who that prowler was. What would we do if he comes back?"

"Just what Officer Steves told us to do,"

Molly said. "We'll call the police again, and let them handle it. All *I* really want to do is catch whoever is messing with my paper!"

# 5

## MENACE ON MAIN STREET

That afternoon, Molly, Susan, Linda, and a dozen other girls gathered at the Red Cross headquarters to finish their friendship bags. For the past several weeks, the JRC girls had been sewing the small cloth bags and filling them with items to brighten a wounded soldier's day: a candy bar, some gum, a small comic book.

After Molly finished her third bag, she drew a picture of herself standing beneath an American flag. Then she wrote "Thank you for defending us!" at the bottom, signed her name with a flourish, and slipped the note into the bag she'd stitched of cheerful red cotton. She reached for another piece of cloth, but there were none left.

"Miss Delaney, I think we're about done!" Molly announced. She looked up expectantly.

Miss Delaney did not appear to have heard. She stood by the window that looked over the street. She had a half-thoughtful, half-sad look on her face.

"Miss Delaney?" Molly tried again.

"What? Oh!" Miss Delaney turned, and her sad look was gone. "I beg your pardon, Molly. My goodness! Are you girls finished already?"

"Yes," Alison Hargate announced. Linda pointed proudly at the friendship bags lined up on the table.

Miss Delaney beamed. "I could not be any prouder of you girls. Molly, tell your father that the Jefferson Junior Red Cross is coming to the hospital on Wednesday to lift some wounded soldiers' spirits."

"I've never been inside a hospital," Susan said slowly. "What do you suppose it will be like?"

"We may see men who have been terribly wounded," Alison Hargate said. She looked a little nervous.

"Or someone crazy," another girl chimed in.

"My dad says that some of the men coming back from the war have gone wacky."

"Gracious, girls!" Miss Delaney said. "There's nothing to worry about. We're going to bring cheer to men who have made enormous sacrifices for our country."

"My dad said the military tries to send soldiers, sailors, and pilots to the hospital that's closest to their home," Molly told her friends. "So we might even see someone we know! And my older sister Jill says the patients are grateful for every kindness."

Miss Delaney spread her arms, as if wanting to hug the whole group. "There now, you see? The men will be glad to see you, I promise. Wear your nicest dresses! Looking pretty for the men is patriotic, too."

After putting the sewing supplies away, Molly, Linda, and Susan waved good-bye to their friends. "Want to say hello to your mother?" Susan asked as they started down the stairs.

"Sure!" Molly said. "Maybe she can even walk home with us."

The girls went downstairs to the main office of the Red Cross. As Molly opened the door, she saw her mother sitting at a desk, talking on a telephone. A dozen people waited in line for Mrs. Fitzgerald, the volunteer coordinator. Molly also recognized Mr. Ellison, who coordinated the Victory garden program, at another desk. He had a radio on his desk and was tapping a pencil in time to the rollicking beat of "Boogie Woogie Bugle Boy." Two teenage girls chattered as they rolled bandages. A lively committee meeting seemed to be taking place in one corner.

Molly caught Mom's eye and waved. Mom waved back and blew Molly a kiss.

"Come on," Molly said. "She's too busy to stop."

Once outside, Susan paused to examine the tip of her forefinger. "I only pricked myself twice today. I'm actually starting to *like* sewing."

Linda jumped down the last three steps. "That's because Miss Delaney makes it fun!"

"Miss Delaney seemed to have something on her mind today," Molly said.

Linda shrugged. "Maybe she's just tired. She works third shift in the factory, like my mom."

"That must be—" Molly began. Her voice died as a man down the street started bellowing. Suddenly the girls were being jostled by pedestrians. The people who had lined up outside the grocery store, hoping there might be a delivery of meat or sugar that afternoon, left their places. People hurried from the post office and the bank.

"What's happening?" Linda cried.

Molly stared at the confusion. "I don't know!"

Then Mr. Ellison burst through the door of the Red Cross building. "It's over in Europe!" he yelled. "I heard it on the radio!"

Molly stared, not sure she understood. It couldn't be. Could it? *Could it?* "What's over?" she demanded.

A huge grin split Mr. Ellison's face. "The war in Europe! The Germans have surrendered!" He pounded on down the steps.

Molly and her friends stared at each other, silent with shock. Then they were hugging and jumping up and down and screaming and laughing and crying, all at once. "The Germans have surrendered!" Molly cried over and over. "The Germans have *surrendered!*"

More people poured out of the Red Cross building. Miss Delaney paused on the top step, her hands clasped, her face alight. Mrs. Fitzgerald's eyes glittered with unshed tears.

When Mom came outside and spotted the girls, she scampered down the steps like a child. "Can you believe it?" she gasped. "Let's stand back out of the way!" She had to yell to be heard.

Molly had never seen anything like this. A boy shimmied up a light pole and waved a flag. Several men began singing "America the Beautiful." A driver honked his horn. A group of teenagers began dancing right in the middle of the street. Two sailors, probably home on leave, kissed every young woman within reach. Someone opened a second-story window and began tossing scraps of paper torn from a telephone directory out like confetti.

# Clues in the Shadows

The day they had all dreamed of, worked for, prayed for, had finally, *finally* come. Victory in Europe. *We beat the German army*, Molly thought, trying to grasp the miraculous news. The war in Europe was *over*. She was content to stand safely against the wall, grinning, watching this miraculous pageant unfold in front of her. This moment was truly special! She could feel that in her heart.

And she could see it, too, on the faces of her friends and neighbors. There was Jimmy Cochran, the soda jerk at the drugstore—his face glowed like a candle. And there was Mrs. Hamilton, who had lost one son in the war and had two more serving in Europe. Her seamed face held a mixture of grief and gratitude and pride. But everyone, *everyone*, was sharing a rare moment of joy—

Suddenly Molly stiffened. No, not everyone. Wasn't that Miss Delaney . . . ? People jostled by, blocking Molly's view. She jerked away from the wall and began to shoulder her way through the crowd.

"Molly!" Mom called.

"I'll be right back!" Molly yelled over her shoulder. She stumbled when a woman with a market basket banged into her. Finally Molly plowed her way to the top of the steps of the Red Cross building. She stood on tiptoe, craning her neck.

Yes—there was Miss Delaney. She no longer looked happy, or even sad-but-proud. Molly couldn't quite read the expression on her friend's face: Was it concern? Worry? Maybe even fright?

Molly hollered "Miss Delaney!" but her voice was lost in the hubbub. Miss Delaney seemed to be staring at something or someone, her eyes still wide and fearful. Molly looked in the same direction, searching the crowd. She saw a father hoist his little girl on top of his shoulders, and a woman wiping away thankful tears with a handkerchief. Then Molly felt a sudden chill as she caught a glimpse of a tall man with carrot-colored hair wearing a blue and brown plaid jacket. Fletcher! He was standing against the grocery store window. Excited people milled past him, but Fletcher stood like a statue.

Molly glanced back toward Miss Delaney. She'd disappeared into the ever-growing crowd.

Trying not to bowl anyone over, Molly plunged back down the steps. "Excuse me," she panted. "Sorry—excuse me, please!" She almost tripped when someone stepped on one of her shoelaces, but she kept moving. No one seemed to mind, or even notice, as she elbowed her way to the place where she'd seen that plaid jacket.

When she reached the spot, he was gone.

*And what would you have done if you'd caught up to him?* she demanded of herself. *Ask him if he'd done something to frighten Miss Delaney?* Molly frowned at the thought, remembering the day the police had arrested Fletcher. Why was Fletcher out of jail, anyway?

Whatever the answer, this man was definitely best left to the police. What *she* needed to do right now was get back to Mom. As Molly crouched to retie her shoelace, she noticed a pile of peanut shells on the sidewalk, already almost covered with shreds of phone-book confetti. She couldn't help wondering if someone was going to sweep up all the scraps for the paper drive once the celebration was over.

"Molly!" Mom cried as she pushed through the crowd with her arms around Susan and Linda. "We need to stay together in this crush!"

"Sorry!" Molly shouted. "It's just that I saw—" She stopped as the bells of the Catholic church down the street began to bong.

"I want to get you girls home," Mom shouted back. She began easing through the celebration like a mother duck with nestlings in tow. Linda and Susan laughed, taking it all in, not minding the jostle and din.

For Molly, though, some of the day's joy had dimmed. She was positive she'd seen Fletcher. She couldn't be sure that it had been Fletcher who had put that troubled look on Miss Delaney's face, not in such a crowd. But it really had looked as if she was staring right at him.

Who was Fletcher, anyway? And what had he done to upset Miss Delaney? Molly felt a

growing sense of unease. Prowlers in the backyard, a strange man arrested for punching someone, the memory of Miss Delaney's worried
expression... In all the years of waiting and
hoping and dreaming about victory in Europe,
Molly had never imagined that the moment
would be shadowed by such troubles.

# 6
## CLUES IN THE SHED

The following day, the students at Molly's school attended a special assembly so that they could celebrate Victory in Europe, honor the soldiers who had died, and—as Miss Delaney had put it—rededicate themselves to continuing the fight to win victory in the Pacific islands. The high-spirited celebration on the street had given way to something quieter, deeper. Molly and her friends agreed to postpone their detective work. Even Ricky didn't tease or pick any quarrels.

That evening the McIntires attended a special service at their church. Men clapped each other on the shoulder. Women reached for friends' hands. The minister's prayers of thanks were moving. Still, Molly felt an ache inside as she

watched Gold Star mothers lighting candles
for their sons who had been killed in battle.
*I just want the **whole** war to be over*, she thought.
*Over for good.*

On Wednesday, life eased back to normal.
After school Molly went downtown again to
collect paper. She rode her bike so that she
could range farther from home, although the
bike's basket didn't hold as much as the baby
carriage. An hour later she wobbled home
with one hand on the handlebars and the other
pressed on the newspapers and other scraps
piled in the basket, trying to keep them from
blowing away.

Dad came out the back door just as Molly
braked to a halt in the driveway. "You've got
quite a haul there," he said. "When do you have
to deliver it?"

Molly got off the bike and set the kickstand.
"The first collection is Friday afternoon," she

told him. "Red Cross volunteers will have scales to weigh everyone's paper."

"I can help you haul what you've gathered," Dad offered. "We can take the LaSalle. We have enough gas coupons for that short trip."

Molly bounced on her toes. "Thanks, Dad!"

"I'm off to the hospital," Dad told her. He put his arm around her shoulders and gave her a squeeze. "Are you heading out on another paper run?"

"No time right now," Molly said. "The JRC girls are visiting the veterans' hospital this afternoon, remember?"

He nodded. "Ah, yes."

"Some of the girls are a little nervous about it," Molly told him. "I think they're afraid of seeing something scary. I mean, we've all seen newsreels of wounded men." Some of the black-and-white films had been difficult to watch.

Dr. McIntire pulled his pipe and the little bag of tobacco from his jacket pocket. "Don't worry, sweetheart. The men you'll be visiting are recuperating well. The scary things..." He paused, striking a match so that he could light the tobacco. "Those things are mostly in hospitals near the fighting."

"One of the girls said some veterans come home with mental problems," Molly said. "Her dad said they'd gone wacky."

Dad looked Molly in the eye. "It's not kind to call people 'wacky,' Molly. Yes, some of the soldiers do come home with nervous problems. I've heard people call it 'the jitters.' We doctors call it 'battle fatigue.' Battle fatigue is a medical condition. Most of the men suffering with it will improve if they get help from doctors who are trained to treat them."

"Oh," Molly said. She thought again about the pictures of fighting men she'd seen in *Life* magazine and in the newsreels that played before feature films. *If I were a soldier,* she thought, *I'd surely come home with the jitters, too.*

Dad's voice softened as he added, "I'm sure your visit will be a big hit."

Molly gave Dad a good-bye hug, then waved

as he walked briskly away. When he was out of sight, she grabbed her bike's handlebars, nudged the kickstand up with her foot, and walked it into the backyard. She was thinking about what Dad had said when a sudden movement caught her eye. She glanced up sharply and saw Ronnie Vanko standing near the property line between her yard and his.

"What do you want?" Molly demanded.

Ronnie scowled. "Nothing." He turned away.

"Wait!" Molly said. "Somebody messed with the paper I collected. If I ever find out—"

"I don't want your stupid old paper!" Ronnie shouted over his shoulder. He ran into his house and slammed the door.

"Yeah," Molly muttered. "Right."

When she opened the shed door, she was pleased to see that her piles of paper were still neatly stacked against the wall. Her DO NOT TOUCH sign was undisturbed, too. *Maybe it did the trick*, she thought.

Molly quickly stacked the newsprint and

brown wrapping paper she'd salvaged that afternoon. She wanted to get to the Red Cross building early, so that she could talk with Miss Delaney before the other girls arrived. But as Molly started to hurry from the shed, something stopped her.

She paused, looking around. The shed's two small windows allowed only dim light, but she didn't see anything out of place. Then she realized that the shed *smelled* different. It still held the sweet mustiness of earth and seed potatoes, and the metallic tang of the oil Mrs. Gilford used to keep trowels and hoe blades from rusting. But drifting behind those was a faint swirl of cigarette smoke.

Molly wrinkled her nose. Who would have smoked in here? Surely not Ricky or Ronnie. Ricky would never do something so stupid. And although Ronnie was lazy and sometimes mean, she didn't think he'd be that dumb, either.

*The prowler had smelled of cigarette smoke.*

That unwanted thought made Molly's mouth

go dry, but she forced herself to think clearly. Why would the prowler be interested in the garden shed? There was nothing here but stacks of waste paper and some everyday garden tools. Besides, lots of adults smoked cigarettes.

Molly poked among the shadows on the floor with the toe of one of her saddle shoes, looking for a discarded cigarette butt. She didn't find one. In the silence, though, she did hear a tiny *crunch.*

Dropping to her knees, Molly moved a shovel so that she could better explore. She found a scrap of string, a few stray garden stakes... and a crushed peanut shell. How did that get in here? The only time Molly had seen peanut shells recently was on the sidewalk in front of the grocery store the day the German surrender had been announced. She'd seen a pile of them at the spot where she'd seen the man in the plaid jacket—Fletcher, who'd been arrested for punching someone at the telephone company. The man who had, she thought, said or done something to upset Miss Delaney.

Molly jumped to her feet and hurried from the shed. Maybe it was all a coincidence.

But if not, what on earth was going on?

When Molly went inside, she passed Mrs. Gilford and Brad in the kitchen without telling them what she'd discovered. She didn't want to worry them.

Then Jill came thumping down the stairs, wearing her nurse's aide uniform. "Jill, listen," Molly began. "I think I smelled cigarette smoke in the garden shed!"

"Some neighbor was probably burning leaves," Jill said. "Now, *you* listen. I need a favor, and I'm in a hurry."

"I know the difference between burning leaves and cigarette smoke!" Molly retorted crossly. She started up the stairs. "And I'm in a hurry too. I've got to—"

"I *know*," Jill interrupted. "You're heading to the Red Cross building, right? I told Mrs.

Fitzgerald that I'd send over the box of costume jewelry I've collected, but I forgot to give it to Mom this morning."

"I'll take it," Molly said. She was already halfway up the stairs.

"It's on my bed," Jill called. "Oh! I almost forgot. Mom said she'd leave a jewelry donation on her bureau."

"O-*kay!*" Molly shouted.

As she quickly washed up and rebraided her hair, she thought through what she'd noticed in the garden shed. Trying to talk with Jill about it had been useless. Mom wouldn't want her to tell Dad, and Mom and Mrs. Gilford probably wouldn't take her seriously, either. Some newspapers strewn about a couple of days ago, a faint whiff of smoke today, a single peanut shell? Everyone was too busy to worry about such things.

*Everyone but me*, Molly thought as she pulled on her prettiest dress. She grabbed Jill's box and hurried to her parents' bedroom. A pair of silver earrings and a bracelet glittering with rhinestones waited on the bureau.

Molly scooped them up and tucked them into the box. Then she noticed several photographs turned upside down on a corner of the bureau. What were pictures doing up here? Mom organized all of the family snapshots into albums that she kept downstairs. Perplexed, Molly picked up the stack and turned them over.

She realized instantly that these were not family photographs. The three men in the first black-and-white photo were dressed in military uniforms. They looked filthy and tired, but they had smiled for the camera. The next photo was a little blurry, but Molly could make out two uniformed men carrying a stretcher.

*These are Dad's pictures!* a voice in her head scolded. *And he did not invite you to snoop!*

Molly glanced up, listening hard. No one was about. She had to look at these photos— she just *had* to. Maybe they would help her understand something of Dad's experiences. And maybe that would help her help *him*.

She took a deep breath and held it, steeling herself to see something scary. Then she looked at the next snapshot.

It was a shock...but not the kind she had expected. Dad, wearing his uniform, was crouching on the ground and grinning at the camera. And one arm was around a dark-haired girl who looked no older than Molly.

Molly stared at the image. The girl was very pretty. But who was she?

# 7

# SURPRISE IN WARD B

Even with all the distractions, Molly managed to get to the Red Cross headquarters fifteen minutes early. She still wanted to talk to Miss Delaney before the other girls arrived. *I'll drop off the jewelry on my way out,* she thought as she hurried up the stairs. She was relieved to find Miss Delaney alone in the meeting room, seated at the worktable.

Miss Delaney looked up from some photographs she had spread out in front of her. "Why, hello, Molly."

Molly couldn't help noticing that her friend's eyes were rimmed with fatigue. "Are you feeling all right?" Molly asked.

"I'm fine," Miss Delaney said. "Just a bit tired."

Molly looked at the photos on the table. Each was a lovely portrait of a mother and baby. "Oh, gosh!" she breathed. "These are terrific!"

Miss Delaney looked pleased. "Those babies were all born after their fathers went overseas. The Red Cross will send these pictures to the dads."

Molly felt a lump in her throat as she thought about what these photographs would mean to homesick soldiers. "They're beautiful," she murmured. "Did you take them?"

"I did," Miss Delaney said. "Before the war, I worked in a photography studio. I love doing these mom and baby portraits. I'm going to do another group next week!" She began gathering the photographs.

Molly remembered why she'd come early. "Miss Delaney," she began, "on Monday, when everyone came outside to celebrate the Germans' surrender . . . well, I happened to notice you in the middle of all that. And suddenly you didn't look happy anymore."

Miss Delaney carefully slid the photographs

into an envelope. "Of course I was happy, Molly. It was joyful news."

"I know, but . . ." Molly hesitated, then came out with it. "You looked scared."

For a moment Miss Delaney stared at the envelope as if it held some secret. Then she looked up. "You must have been mistaken, dear."

Molly didn't think she was mistaken.

Miss Delaney tipped her head. "Come sit down, Molly. At the moment, *you* look like you're unhappy about something. Is everything all right?"

"I don't know." Molly slid into a chair. "I saw a man get arrested last week. And I thought I saw him again on Monday when everyone crowded into the street."

Surprise flickered briefly in Miss Delaney's eyes. "Well, that must have been upsetting," she murmured. "But I'm sure the police wouldn't release a true troublemaker, so there's nothing to worry about."

Molly smoothed a wrinkle in her dress. Thoughts of peanut shells and prowlers and a photograph of Dad with a mystery girl swirled in her mind.

"Molly?" Miss Delaney asked gently. "Is something else troubling you?"

"Well...I'm a little worried about my dad," Molly confessed. "He hasn't been quite himself since he got home."

"Perhaps he's still adjusting to being home," Miss Delaney said. "It might help if he talks about his experiences."

"But that's just it!" Molly said. "He won't talk to me about his time in England." She put one elbow on the table and propped her cheek on her hand. "He brought home some—"

A burst of excited laughter drifted into the room. Miss Delaney's eyes were warm with sympathy as she squeezed Molly's hand. "Give him time," she said. "Sometimes that's all you can do."

Susan and Linda burst through the door, followed by Alison and several other girls. Miss Delaney got up to greet them. *I came here to talk about her worries, and we ended up talking about mine instead*, Molly realized. That was just like Miss Delaney.

All the girls looked their best. Alison looked particularly lovely in a spring-green sweater.

"Is that a new outfit?" Susan asked Alison. "It sure is pretty!"

"It is new," Alison confided. When she twisted a little, letting her gray skirt swish back and forth, Molly noticed a gold brooch in the shape of a bird pinned to her sweater. A tiny blue stone that formed the bird's eye twinkled.

"There's a jewelry drive on," Molly said. Her voice came out a little louder than she'd intended.

Alison looked startled. "I know. A couple of high-school girls came to our door. Mother and I gave them quite a few pieces to send to the soldiers." She touched the bird pin on her shoulder. "I saved this one to wear to the hospital, to help cheer up the wounded."

Susan leaned close to Molly. "What's the matter?" she whispered.

"Nothing," Molly whispered back. "I just

have to drop off this box downstairs for Jill."

"We'll meet you by the front door!" Susan called after her. Molly raised a hand to show that she'd heard.

Halfway down the stairs, Molly's steps slowed, then stopped. She had worn her favorite dress, but it was two years old, and looked it. She stared at the box in her hands, glanced over her shoulder at the empty stairwell, and then eased off the box lid. Mom's donations lay on top of a jumble of pins and earrings and bracelets. Most were inexpensive pieces made pretty with rhinestones and bits of brightly colored glass. An enameled pin shaped like a rose caught Molly's eye, and she fished it out. It wouldn't do any harm to borrow it, would it? Just for today, while visiting the wounded soldiers. Then she'd pass it on to Mrs. Fitzgerald.

With the red rose pin glittering on her dress, Molly ran the rest of the way down the stairs.

# CLUES IN THE SHADOWS

The Jefferson veterans' hospital had windows overlooking gardens bursting with daffodils and tulips. Cheerful paintings hung on corridor walls. The faint sounds of a guitar being played drifted down the hallway. Still, Molly did feel a little nervous as the JRC girls, clutching their sacks of friendship bags, waited for instructions near the entryway.

"I wish Miss Delaney had come," she whispered to Susan and Linda. She'd been surprised to learn that Mrs. Gallagher, another Red Cross volunteer, was going to shepherd the girls along instead.

Now Mrs. Gallagher clapped her hands. "This way, girls," she called. "We're going to Ward B."

Molly and her friends silently followed Mrs. Gallagher into a large room. Wounded soldiers were lying down or sitting propped against pillows in beds lining the two long walls. Some men had arms or legs in plaster casts. Others were missing an arm or a leg.

Molly swallowed hard. What was she going to say to these heroes?

"Good afternoon," Mrs. Gallagher called. "You have some visitors from the Junior Red Cross." Then she leaned down and whispered, "Go ahead, girls!"

Molly walked slowly to one of the beds. The man there had a bandage wrapped around one shoulder. "Hello," she said uncertainly. "My name is Molly McIntire. I brought you this." She put one of her little bags on the bed.

"Thanks," the young man said politely. He picked up the bag and peered inside. Suddenly his face lit up. "Golly!" he exclaimed, pulling out a comic book. "Joe Palooka! My *favorite!*"

After that, Molly found it easier to approach each patient. Some men were shy, but they all seemed grateful for the goodies in the friendship bags.

Then one young man met her cheerful greeting with a gasp of dismay. "Is something wrong?" Molly faltered, feeling her confidence wobble.

"Oh—sorry," he said. Smiling, he extended a hand for her to shake. "My name's Billy. I didn't mean to be rude. It's just that your pin looks exactly like one I sent to a girl I used to know. I bought it in France. Where did you get yours?"

"Um, actually, it's not mine," Molly stammered. "I just borrowed it." She touched the enameled rose, feeling her cheeks grow warm with embarrassment. *Serves you right for borrowing something without permission,* she scolded herself. But who could have guessed that the pin she had hoped would help cheer up soldiers would end up prompting a frown instead?

Eager to change the subject, she hastily handed Billy a friendship bag. "This is for you."

Billy was delighted to find two of Mrs. Petroski's gingersnaps in his bag. "Ah," he said happily. "Thanks a lot. This is really swell."

"You must have missed home-cooked food while you were overseas," Molly said.

"I did," Billy said simply. "I don't have any family, so I didn't have as much to lose as most of these guys." He gestured widely at his comrades. "But when I was slogging through France and Holland, scared and filthy and tired, I dreamed about cookies like these. Oh, and my dog."

"Who's taking care of your dog?" Molly asked.

Billy's face clouded. "A neighbor took care of Rex, for a while. But Rex was really old. He died before I got home."

"Oh no," Molly said. On top of everything else Billy had been through, Rex's death seemed horribly unfair. "I'm really sorry. I have a dog too, so I can imagine how you feel."

"Tell me about your dog," Billy said. "Does he come running to you when you get home? Rex always did that."

Molly perched on the side of the bed and soon had Billy laughing about the time Bennett had rolled in muddy water, then shaken himself to dry—right beside the clothesline where Jill was hanging clean sheets. And as she finished, Molly got an idea. A *fantastic* idea. She smiled, imagining how much fun it would be to follow through with the plan. All she needed was Dad's permission. *I'll talk to him as soon as I can,* she thought.

"What else do you like to do?" Billy asked.

"Well, I'm a tap dancer," Molly told him. "I got to be Miss Victory in a pageant."

Billy smiled. "I wish I could have seen that!"

"I can show you a few steps," Molly offered. She didn't have her music or her glittering costume or her special tap shoes, but she decided that those things didn't really matter.

When Molly began to dance, the men nearby stopped chatting to watch. Soon the room was quiet. Then someone started clapping to help her keep time, and everyone joined in. A few men from nearby wards crowded into the room. When she finished, the room exploded in cheers and applause. The men who were able to leave their beds crowded around her.

"That was great!"

"You remind me of my kid sister!"

"One day I'll be able to dance again, too!"

*I'm so glad we came!* Molly thought. As she and the other girls moved from soldier to soldier, thanking them and saying good-bye, she felt ready to burst with pride. All she had to offer these brave men were friendship bags and a tap dance and her gratitude. She was thankful that she had been able to lift their spirits, even if just for a little while.

If only Miss Delaney had been there to share the visit! Then it would have been perfect.

# 8
## THE GREAT GIRL DETECTIVE

When Molly got home, Mom was preparing a late supper of cheese sandwiches and tomato soup. "How was your trip to the veterans' hospital?" she asked.

"It went great!" Molly said. "I think the soldiers were glad we came."

Mom turned down the heat beneath the soup so that it wouldn't scorch. "And I'll bet your friendship bags were a real hit," she said.

"They were." Molly began to get dishes out so she could set the table. "But you know what? I think what made the soldiers happiest was just having a chance to talk to someone new."

"Sometimes the best gift you can give someone is a listening ear," Mom said.

Molly nodded. "I just hope Miss Delaney goes

with us next time. She's *always* a good listener."

"Miss Delaney?" Mom looked startled. "Didn't she tell you?"

"Tell me what?" Molly began to fold a napkin into a neat triangle.

Mom put her spoon down. "Oh dear. Molly, Miss Delaney resigned from her volunteer work at the Red Cross."

The napkin fell to the table. "*What?* When did she do that?"

"Right after you girls left with Mrs. Gallagher. I just assumed that she'd already said good-bye to all of you."

Molly sank into a chair. "But—but why? Did she say why she was quitting?"

"She said that her volunteer work, on top of her job at the factory, was getting to be too much," Mom said. "No one was expecting it. Although..." She sighed. "The war in the Pacific could last a long time, I'm afraid. People are simply getting weary."

Molly folded her arms, feeling hurt and angry. *I'm tired too*, she thought. *But I would never*

*quit a job without saying good-bye to my friends.*
And what about the portraits of mothers and
new babies? Miss Delaney had another session
scheduled for next week!

Molly frowned. This didn't make any sense.
Miss Delaney had spoken eagerly of taking more
portraits. Fifteen minutes later, after the girls
left for the veterans' hospital, Miss Delaney had
quit her volunteer work. Why? What had made
Miss Delaney decide to resign?

*The only thing that happened in those fifteen
minutes*, Molly thought, *is that Miss Delaney talked
to me.* Miss Delaney had listened to Molly's concern about Dad, but that wouldn't be any reason
for her to leave the Red Cross. The only other
topic of conversation had been Fletcher. There
*must* be some trouble between Fletcher and Miss
Delaney—some problem that Miss Delaney was
afraid to even discuss.

Molly felt a little clutch in her chest. She'd
been trying to help Miss Delaney by asking her
about Fletcher. Somehow, though, that had gone
terribly wrong.

Molly was quiet during supper. After the dishes were washed, she headed upstairs and retrieved the rose pin from the drawer where she'd tucked it earlier. She wanted to talk to Jill, privately.

Five minutes later, though, Ricky burst into the room. "You little sneak," he said angrily. "How could you?"

"How could I *what?*"

"You know what!" he said. "You were messing with my paper!"

"Your paper?" she echoed. "Someone got into the paper you collected?"

Ricky glared at her. "Don't act so innocent. I was just in the garage. Someone knocked my stacks of paper over. Did you think you could steal some?"

"No!" Molly insisted. "In fact—"

*"Stop it!"* Jill's voice was low and full of warning. She stood in the doorway, but quickly came inside and closed the door behind her.

"What is the matter with you two? Dad's downstairs! Do you want him to know you're fighting?"

"No," Ricky and Molly muttered at the same time.

"You both need to grow up," Jill scolded. "Honestly!"

"But—" Molly began.

"You're right," Ricky interrupted, looking at Jill. Then he fixed Molly with an accusing look. "But I mean it, Molly. If you ever mess up my paper again, or steal some so you can get more credit, you'll be in *big* trouble." With that he stormed out of the bedroom—but quietly, so as not to disturb Dad.

Molly sank onto the bed. "I didn't touch his paper!" she told Jill. "Really! In fact, someone has been messing with *my* paper." If it wasn't Ricky, that left Ronnie Vanko as the only likely culprit.

Jill sighed. "This whole thing is out of hand. I'm starting to think that awarding the Eisenhower medals is a bad idea. All it's done is get you kids wound up."

"I'm not wound up!" Molly protested. She could tell, though, that Jill didn't want to hear any more about the paper drive. "Jill? I wanted to ask you about something else." She held the rose pin toward her sister. "Do you remember where you got this?"

"Molly!" Jill crossed her arms, looking more disapproving than ever. "What are you doing with that? You were supposed to—"

"I just borrowed it," Molly interrupted. She quickly told Jill about meeting Billy. "Do you remember who donated this pin?"

"Well . . . yes, I do." Jill hesitated before saying, "It was Darleen Delaney."

"Miss Delaney quit?" Susan gasped, just as Linda said, "I don't believe it."

"It's true," Molly said. The girls had agreed to meet at Linda's house that evening, and they were in her bedroom. After flopping onto the bed, Molly shared what Mom and Jill had told her about Miss Delaney.

"I can't believe she didn't even say good-bye," Susan said.

"I can't either," Molly said. "That's why I think Miss Delaney must be having some kind of trouble. She'd never leave like that if she wasn't."

"That Fletcher guy must be bothering her for some reason," Linda said grimly.

"We should go visit her," Susan said. "Do you know where she lives?"

Molly shook her head. "No. Jill said Miss Delaney had that pin tucked away in her purse, and she gave it to Jill at the Red Cross building."

Susan slouched in her chair. "Now we'll probably never know what Miss Delaney's secret is."

"I'm not ready to give up," Molly said stubbornly. "Miss Delaney works at the airplane factory, right?"

Linda nodded. "On the night shift."

"Okay, then, here's my plan," Molly said. "Tomorrow morning, we get up early and ride our bikes to the factory. We can wait by the gate until the night-shift workers come through. When we see Miss Delaney, we'll tell her that we're worried. We can try to convince her to go to the police if Fletcher is making trouble for her." She looked at her friends triumphantly, expecting them to agree that she'd come up with a brilliant plan.

Instead, Linda shook her head. "I can't leave early. I've got to watch Joey."

"And I can't either," Susan said. "Mom's been quizzing me on history every morning, half an hour before breakfast."

"Oh." Molly's shoulders sagged. "I guess I'll have to go by myself."

"Sorry, Molly." Susan glanced out the window, then stood up. "It's going to be dark soon. I've got to get home."

"Me too," Molly said. She thought of the prowler and shivered.

"I've got a box of paper in the garage for you," Linda told her. "You might as well take it now."

Molly and Susan followed her outside to the garage. When Linda pointed at the box, Molly leaned over to pick it up. "Wait!" Linda said suddenly.

Molly froze. "What's the matter?"

"This isn't how I left it," Linda said. She crouched by the open carton and began pawing through its contents: several newspapers, some odd pieces of notebook paper, a couple of envelopes. "When I carried the box out, a folded newspaper was on top," she told her friends. "I did that on purpose because I didn't want any of the smaller pieces to blow away. But now these old envelopes are on top."

"Ronnie Vanko!" Molly muttered. "When I catch him—"

"No, that's not it," Linda said. "Nothing is *missing*. Someone pawed through all this stuff but didn't take anything."

The girls stared at each other. "This is getting creepy," Susan said nervously.

Molly thought so too. "I just figured that Ricky or Ronnie wanted to sabotage my collection so they could get a medal," she said slowly. "But that doesn't seem to be what's going on. Nothing's missing! Someone just messed up my piles of paper, and the same thing happened to Ricky."

"Somebody must be *looking* for something," Linda said.

Molly looked from one friend to the other. "We've got a Paper Prowler on our hands."

"Kids are picking up scrap paper all over town," Susan pointed out. "Maybe someone put something important into a pile by mistake, and now he's trying to find it."

"But if that's the case, why sneak around?" Linda demanded. "Why not just put a notice in the newspaper or something, asking kids to look for whatever is missing?"

"There's only one good reason to sneak around," Molly said. "The missing papers must have to do with something...something *bad*."

"Like what?" Linda asked. "What could be so horrible?"

Molly tried to think. "Well, Mrs. Gilford

mentioned that someone in town is trying to pass off counterfeit ration coupons. What if one of us picked up a stack of paper that contained pages of fake coupons? If we had noticed, and remembered where that stack had come from, it might have helped the police arrest the counterfeiter."

Susan's eyes went wide. "Or maybe some spy wrote a letter, and it got put into a scrap pile! Remember when the war started, and people got suspicious of neighbors who had German names? Most of that was just meanness, but maybe there really is a spy in Jefferson!"

Molly didn't like any of these ideas. Each one sent a new little shiver tingling down her back. And when she glanced outside, she also didn't like how the evening's gloom had deepened into nearly full darkness. "We've got to get going," she said. "But remember, we're all going to watch for a prowler in our yards tonight." Since their neighborhood watch had been postponed by the Victory in Europe celebration, Molly didn't want to let another evening slip by.

"I don't know," Susan said slowly. "Don't you think we should call the police about the Paper Prowler?"

"But we don't have any real evidence of a crime!" Molly protested. "If we keep watch tonight, maybe we'll learn something important."

"I think we should keep all of this a secret until we figure it out," Linda agreed. She made a quick locking gesture in front of her mouth. "Remember, loose lips can sink ships. If the Paper Prowler hears about our suspicions, he might stay away."

"Okay, you're probably right." Susan sighed. "I'll watch for a while."

"Me too," Linda said.

"Officer Steves said to turn on a light or make some noise if something scary happens," Molly reminded them. "Those things will chase a prowler away."

She hoped they wouldn't have to do that, though. She didn't want the Paper Prowler scared away. She wanted him *caught*.

# Clues in the Shadows

That night, after everyone had gone to sleep, Molly crept down the stairs. Bennett came to greet her in the kitchen, tail thumping happily. "*Shh,*" she whispered as she shrugged into a jacket. "Sorry, boy, but you have to stay inside. Good dog." Clutching a flashlight in one hand, she eased the back door open and slipped outside.

Molly was glad she'd brought a folded towel to sit on, because the concrete steps were cold. For a while she sat rigid, staring at the night. It was a little spooky to be outside all alone. A three-quarter moon was high in the sky, though, and once her eyes adjusted, she could actually see fairly well. The garage was clear among the shadows, and so was the garden shed, and the row of lilac bushes marking the line between her backyard and Ronnie Vanko's.

As the minutes ticked on...and on... Molly found herself slumping sleepily against the back wall. *Maybe this wasn't such a great idea,* she thought. It had been exciting to think about detective work, but she'd had a long, tiring day. And she had plans to get up extra-early in the morning so that she could be at the airplane factory gate when Miss Delaney finished her shift—

Then she heard a sound. Her heart seemed to quicken its beat as she listened. Nothing. Had she imagined it? No, there it was again. The tiniest rustle of sound came from her right. A footstep?

Yes, she was sure of it. Someone was walking between the McIntires' house and Mrs. Petroski's. Someone moving very slowly, very stealthily. Someone headed toward the McIntires' backyard. Any second now, the prowler would come into view. Molly was afraid to move. She clutched the flashlight with an iron grip as her palms slicked with sweat. She hadn't turned the light on, but she might need to.

One more hushed, careful footstep, and the figure came into sight—no more than a silhouette against the night sky. Molly's thoughts jumped like popping corn. Should she scream? Stay still and silent, and watch? Try to follow the person? Run inside and call the police, and hope like crazy that someone would come?

Then she realized something surprising. She had expected to see a repeat visitor—Fletcher, tall and smelling of cigarette smoke. But Molly could tell that this prowler was a different person. Shorter. Much shorter. And stooped. It looked as if the prowler was leaning on a cane. In fact...

Molly's mouth opened in astonishment. Then she stood and crept closer. "Mrs. Petroski?" she hissed. "Is that you?"

"Oh!" Molly's neighbor let loose an exclamation of fright before clapping her hand over her mouth. *"Molly?"* she whispered back. "You frightened me half to death!"

Molly put a warning hand in the air as she looked back at her house. No lights flipped on, no windows banged open. No one had heard them. "Yes, it's me," she said, keeping her voice low. "You scared me, too! What are you doing out here?"

"I—I . . ." Mrs. Petroski's voice quavered. "It's Marmalade, you see. She's run away. I didn't realize she was gone until I got up to get a drink of water."

"Don't you have a flashlight?"

Mrs. Petroski sounded ready to cry. "Well, I do, but I was afraid that if I turned it on, someone would see it and think I was a prowler!"

Molly wanted to smack her palm against her forehead. So much for Molly McIntire, the great girl detective! "Come on," she whispered. "I have a flashlight, too. Everyone's asleep. I'll help you look for Marmalade."

Using their lights, they made a quick search of the McIntires' backyard. There was no sign of Marmalade. "I'm sorry," Molly told her friend. "Maybe she'll come back in the morning."

"Yes, I'm sure she will. Thank you, dear. I'm going back to bed now."

Molly watched her neighbor walk slowly back home. She hoped Marmalade *did* come back, and soon. Mrs. Petroski would be heartbroken if the cat had truly disappeared.

Then Molly blew out a long, disappointed breath. If the Paper Prowler had been lurking nearby, he was probably miles away now! She could only hope that Linda's or Susan's watch had been more successful.

# 9
# FIGHT AT THE FACTORY

Very early the next morning, Molly tiptoed groggily down the stairs. She really, *really* wanted to crawl back to bed. She could get another hour or so of sleep before getting ready for school. *But I have to go look for Miss Delaney*, she told herself. *Maybe I can figure out a way to help her, or convince her to talk to someone else who could.*

She was surprised to smell coffee and to find Dad sitting at the table. He was knitting, with a cup of coffee steaming beside him. "Good morning," she said.

"Oh!" Dad almost dropped his ball of yellow yarn. "You startled me, Molly! I didn't expect to see anyone else up so early." He settled back in his chair. "Hand me the armored cow, will you?"

Molly blinked. *"What?"*

Dad waved a hand. "Sorry. That's what soldiers call canned milk, which is often all they have. The troops use slang words and odd phrases for lots of things. I just want the cream."

"Oh." Molly passed him the pitcher before reaching for the cereal box. "Why are you up?"

"I couldn't sleep," Dad admitted. His tone was light, but Molly saw how he focused intently on his knitting. Even a few days ago, Molly would have given him a bear hug and tried to bring a smile to his face. But now, she hesitated. There was so much she didn't know about his time in England. About the people in the snapshots he'd brought home from the war. About the girl in the photograph—the one who looked a little like her. But she didn't want to admit that she'd snooped.

"And I'm on the early shift," Dad added.

Molly slid into her chair. "You've been working really long hours."

"I'm afraid so," Dad agreed. "And when I've finished my rounds today, I'm meeting with some men who have battle fatigue." He sipped his coffee. "By the way, I heard wonderful things about the JRC visit."

"It was fun," Molly said. "And Dad? A soldier named Billy got me to thinking." She told Dad about the idea she'd gotten while visiting the veterans' hospital.

Dad put aside his knitting and leaned back in his chair. His smile was *almost* bright enough to be called a grin. "Molly, that's a fine plan! You have my full approval."

"Great!" she exclaimed. She wriggled to her feet and put the cereal bowl in the sink. "I'll come by the hospital right after school. Now, I've got to get going! Tell Mom I've already left, okay? Then I won't have to leave a note."

"Sure—but where are you going so early?"

"War work!" Molly called as she darted out the back door.

The airplane factory was on the outskirts of Jefferson, just beyond the railroad station.

The streets were almost deserted as Molly rode her bike west along Illinois Boulevard. Jimmy Cochran was sweeping the sidewalk in front of the drugstore. She passed the milkman as he slowly pedaled his delivery bike down the road, the glass bottles of milk carefully packed into baskets. And when she swerved to give wide clearance to a bus rumbling past, she was surprised to catch a glimpse of someone walking along the railroad tracks.

*That's dangerous!* she thought, braking to a halt. Why would anyone go near the tracks?

Molly lost sight of the figure as it moved behind a row of trees that marched tidily between the street and the railroad tracks, but a moment later the person moved back into view. She blinked. It was Ronnie Vanko! He was walking slowly along the tracks, head bent. He carried a burlap sack over one shoulder. Every now and again he leaned over, picked something up, and stuffed it into the sack.

Was he after paper? He must be. He wouldn't be able to pull his wagon along the rough gravel and railroad ties, which explained the sack. Surely he wouldn't find more than a few scraps along the tracks! Still, every scrap counted.

For a moment Molly's eyes narrowed with frustration. She'd been so busy with the JRC and with worrying about Fletcher and Miss Delaney that her own efforts to collect paper had gotten pushed to the background. The thought of not winning a medal—especially if Ronnie did!—made her mad. *The other things I'm doing are more important*, she reminded herself. The time she spent trying to help Miss Delaney, and visiting the hospital, mattered more than anything else. Still, it was hard not to grumble as she pedaled on down the street. She *did* really want to earn one of those medals.

The airplane factory was a huge facility. Molly had no idea which building Linda's mother and Miss Delaney worked in. The factory had very tight security, though. A tall fence enclosed the entire compound. Linda had told her that all employees had to exit through the same gate.

Molly quickly found a gate, but she didn't

know if it was the right one. A security guard stood inside the gate, but he was too far away to ask. She checked her watch—still early. She decided to keep riding and make sure there wasn't a different gate farther along.

Fifteen minutes later, she was convinced that the first gate was the one she wanted. As Molly pedaled back, she saw that a small crowd had gathered. Most were men—probably fathers waiting to walk their daughters home, or husbands meeting their wives. Molly got off her bike and leaned it against the fence.

"Here they come," a man near her murmured. A stream of workers in stained clothes had appeared between two of the buildings, heading for the gate. Most were women.

Was Miss Delaney in that bunch? Molly stood on tiptoe. Then a man stepped in front of her, completely blocking her view.

Molly darted around behind the crowd, hoping she could get a better look from the other side. Yes! Miss Delaney *was* coming, wearing a cheerful green bandanna with her greasy overalls.

And—there was Linda's mom, too. Molly hoped she could talk to Miss Delaney without having to explain everything to Mrs. Rinaldi.

The waiting crowd shifted as the first women walked through the gate. Molly was forced back a few steps, and she lost sight of Miss Delaney. Well, no matter. In a few moments Miss Delaney would pass through and—

Molly's thought screeched to a halt. There was Fletcher!

He leaned idly against the fence, one foot on the ground, the other braced against the iron rails. Two other men, one stout and one skinny, stood chatting nearby. Fletcher showed no sign of being part of their conversation. He was so close to Molly that when he reached into his pocket, she could see the peanuts he withdrew. He cracked them between his fingers, let the shells fall, popped the nuts into his mouth, munched.

Then, with no warning, Fletcher sprang away from the fence and turned on the stout man. "Shut your fat mouth!" he yelled.

The man stumbled back a few steps. "What the—who *are* you?"

Fletcher's hands closed into fists. He muttered something that Molly couldn't hear. It must not have been nice, because the skinny man flew at Fletcher and knocked him off his feet.

"Fight! Fight!" someone yelled. A woman shrieked. The crowd surged like an ocean swell. Molly struggled between two opposing currents as some people elbowed forward to watch the fight and others tried to slide toward the street. She yelped when someone stepped on her toes. She might have fallen if someone else hadn't been standing so close behind her.

Then a whistle shrilled as one of the factory's security guards came running. "Break it up!" he roared. "And the rest of you—stand back!" He was so commanding that everyone obeyed. The guard grabbed Fletcher with one hand and the skinny man with the other.

Molly's heart was pounding, as if she'd been the one getting yelled at. What was the *matter* with Fletcher? He'd already been arrested for throwing a punch at the telephone company—why pick another fight?

"Who started it?" the guard demanded.

"He did," the skinny man panted, glaring at Fletcher.

"No, *he* started it," Fletcher growled. He jerked his head at the stout man. "He—"

"All right, all right," the guard said. "Do I need to call the police, or will you two clowns knock it off?"

"You can't let him go!" Molly cried. Her cheeks flushed as everyone turned to stare at her. She tried to sound calm and mature as she pointed at Fletcher. "That man got arrested last week for starting a fight. I don't know why the police let him go, but he belongs in jail!"

"No he doesn't!"

All heads swiveled again as Ronnie shoved his way through the crowd. Molly's eyes went wide. Ronnie knew Fletcher?

Ronnie didn't stop until he'd reached Fletcher. "Please don't call the police," he told the guard urgently. "Please, sir. It's all right. He'll be all right."

At that, all the fight seemed to go out of Fletcher. His shoulders slumped. He hung his head.

"Well..." The security guard considered, then looked at the two men Fletcher had confronted. "Anybody want to press charges?"

The stout man hesitated before shaking his head. "No. Forget about it." Then he glared at Fletcher. "But if that nut ever comes near me again, I'll see him behind bars."

The guard released his grip. Ronnie tugged Fletcher's arm, and the two turned away. Ronnie paused just long enough to throw one last look over his shoulder at Molly, his eyes narrowed and dark with anger, and maybe with something else too, something she couldn't name. It took all her courage not to look away.

Ronnie and Fletcher disappeared down the sidewalk. Most of the crowd had dispersed. All of the night-shift workers had left the factory grounds. The security guard pulled the heavy gate closed with a clang and locked it behind him. Only then did Molly remember the errand that had brought her here in the first place—Miss Delaney!

Molly quickly looked around. She ran a few paces down the sidewalk, searching ahead and behind. No sign of a pretty green bandanna. No sign of Miss Delaney.

Darn it! Molly clenched her fists. Nothing was working out the way she'd planned! Fletcher had put a fright into her. Ronnie, the meanest kid in her class *and* her archrival, somehow *knew* Fletcher. And Miss Delaney had disappeared.

Well, nothing could be done about any of that right now. If she didn't get going, she'd be late for school again. Molly fetched her bike and turned back toward town.

Then she spotted something that had been abandoned near the factory fence: a burlap sack. Ronnie must have dropped it when he'd come running to help Fletcher. *I should just leave it,* she thought crossly. If Ronnie didn't get credit for whatever scrap paper he'd collected that morning, that was just too bad.

She couldn't do it, though. Whatever he'd collected belonged to the army and to all the soldiers who desperately needed it. With a heavy sigh, Molly set her kickstand again and went to get the sack. It wasn't very full—there was just a bit of lumpiness in the bottom. She could carry the sack in her bike basket. She didn't feel like giving it back to Ronnie, but maybe she could just hurl the stupid thing into his backyard.

Grabbing the burlap, she started to swing the bag up from the ground. It was so much heavier than she'd expected that she almost knocked her bike over.

*What in the world?* Molly wondered. She opened the bag and peered inside. Then she reached inside. When she pulled her hand out again, it was streaked black. Not ink-black, either. Soot-black.

Ronnie Vanko hadn't been collecting paper at all. Ronnie Vanko had been gathering coal.

# 10
## AN UNEXPECTED VISITOR

Molly dreaded having to sit beside Ronnie in school all day. Ronnie, though, didn't come to school. *Where is he?* Molly wondered. *And how does he know Fletcher?* She didn't find an answer to those questions. About the coal, though... she did have an idea about that. A troubling one.

Molly didn't have a chance to talk with Susan and Linda until they went outside for recess. When the rest of the girls started a dodgeball game, Molly and her friends retreated to one side of the schoolyard.

Susan burst out, "You won't believe what *happened* last night!"

"I've been dying to tell you what *happened* last night!" Linda said at the same time.

Everyone, it turned out, had experienced

some adventure while keeping watch. Linda had heard strange noises one yard over. When she dared creep closer for a good look, she discovered her neighbor digging a hole in the moonlight. "For a moment I thought I'd caught the Paper Prowler," she said. "But he was just trying to dig up a can of gasoline that he'd buried when the war started."

"Why'd he do that?" Susan asked.

"He was hoarding it," Linda said. "When he heard that gasoline was going to be rationed, he filled several cans and buried them. But the cans rusted, and most of the gas leaked out."

"Well, that's what he gets for trying to hoard it," Molly said.

"For a minute I thought I'd caught the Paper Prowler, too," Susan told them. "I was sitting on my back steps, and all of a sudden I heard whispered voices!" She shivered at the memory. "I was just about to run inside and call the police when I recognized one of the voices. It was Brenda, who lives down the street. Remember? She used to be my babysitter."

Molly nodded.

"Well, Brenda works at the factory. Now that the war in Europe is over and the government doesn't need so many planes, some of the women are worried about losing their jobs. So they've started having secret union meetings, trying to figure out how to keep them."

"But the soldiers coming back from the war need those jobs!" Linda protested.

Susan shrugged. "I'm just telling you what Brenda told me."

"I heard something last night, too," Molly said. "But it didn't have anything to do with the war." She told them about Mrs. Petroski, searching for Marmalade.

The girls looked at each other. "I guess we're not the best detectives in the world," Susan said.

"We didn't catch who we were looking for, but I think we did a pretty good job," Linda said. "Who would have guessed that so many people would be creeping around at night?"

A ball escaped the dodgeball court and bounced their way. Molly tossed it back. "I'm

not giving up on identifying the Paper Prowler, though. But *listen*, I have more to tell you—"
A bell rang before Molly could tell them about her morning. Was recess over already? "Darn! I'm going back to the veterans' hospital right after I get home from school. I have the very best idea *ever* for cheering up the veterans. Want to come?"

"We can't," Susan reminded her. "Linda and I have JFA refresher class." Both girls had volunteered for the Junior First Aid program.

"Let's meet at my house this evening," Linda said. "Say, seven o'clock?" Susan nodded.

"I'll be there," Molly promised. Her news about Ronnie and Fletcher would just have to wait. And by seven o'clock, she could report to her friends about her hospital visit, too!

By the time Molly got to the veterans' hospital, her frustration had given way to excitement. "Ready, boy?" she whispered to Bennett. "Let's go make some friends."

When she walked into the ward, leading Bennett on his leash, a ripple of excitement swept the room. Men grinned. "Here, boy!" someone called.

Molly gave them all a big wave. "This is Bennett," she called. "My dad, Dr. McIntire, said it would be okay to bring him for a visit. Don't worry, we'll stop to see everyone!"

The men were delighted to see Bennett. They stroked him, hugged him, told him about their own pets. Many of the men seemed to find it easier to talk when they had a hand resting on the dog. Some told Molly what they wanted to do when they were released from the hospital. Others told her about their sisters, or wives, or children.

Then Molly reached Billy. "Good dog," he said happily as Molly eased Bennett down on the bed beside him. Billy laughed when Bennett licked his hand. "Oh, good boy. Say, Molly, this is just aces. You and Bennett make me really glad I didn't buy the farm."

"What?" Molly exclaimed. That was the second time she'd heard that phrase lately. "You wanted to buy a farm?"

"No!" Billy shuddered. "'Buying the farm' means getting killed in action."

"Oh my gosh!" Molly looked away for a moment. She'd never heard that before, but she remembered Dad saying that soldiers used their own slang phrases for things. And she remembered what Fletcher had said as the police dragged him away: *I might as well have bought the farm, for all that anybody—* Anybody *what?* She'd have to think about that later.

"Bennett sure is a great dog," Billy was saying.

Molly was glad that Bennett was such a hit! She still had something else on her mind, though. Billy had told her that he'd sent a rose pin to a girl. Jill said Miss Delaney had donated the rose pin to the jewelry drive. Molly wanted to ask Billy about Miss Delaney, but she didn't know how to bring up her question without sounding as if she was prying.

"Say," Billy said, "would you like to see a

picture of Rex? It's in the top drawer there."
He gestured at the nightstand beside the bed.

Molly opened the drawer and saw the snapshot right away. It was creased and stained,
and she guessed that Billy had carried it in his
uniform pocket. She smiled at the image of a
younger Billy, sitting beside a big German shepherd who seemed to be grinning at the camera.
"Rex must have been a great pal," she said. She
reached for the picture, wanting to get a closer
look at Rex. She realized a moment too late that
she'd actually picked up two photographs, one
beneath the other. The second snapshot fluttered
to the bed.

"Sorry," Molly said. "I didn't mean to..."
Her voice trailed away as she picked up the
second picture. It was a bit tattered as well, and
showed Billy in a crisply pressed army uniform.
Posed beside him, smiling at the camera, was
Miss Darleen Delaney.

"Oh—that." Billy took the picture from
Molly. His joyful grin faded to a smile, half sad
and half sweet.

"Billy," Molly began. "Is that the girl you gave the rose pin to?"

"Yeah." He handed the snapshot back to her. "Darleen Delaney was one sweet gal."

So Miss Delaney *had* gotten the rose pin from Billy! Could Billy be the reason that Miss Delaney hadn't come to the veterans' hospital with the JRC girls? Did they have some tragic history of a failed romance? Finally Molly asked, "Was Miss Delaney your girlfriend?"

"Well..." Billy looked a little embarrassed. "No. She was a camera girl."

Molly's forehead wrinkled. "A camera girl?"

"Sure," Billy said. "Lots of the nightclub owners hired camera girls when the war began. Did you ever hear of the Lucky Diamond? It's downtown. That's where Darleen worked."

"I don't understand," Molly said.

Bennett had rolled blissfully onto his back. Billy scratched the dog's chest. "It was her job to take pictures, right there in the nightclub. A lot of the guys posed with their wives or their girl-friends. They wanted a picture to take overseas."

Molly *still* didn't understand. "So were you and Miss Delaney a couple back then?"

"Naw. I was having a drink one night, right before shipping out. This pretty camera girl asked me if I'd like a photograph to take with me. I'd been watching her take pictures of couples all evening, and I told her I didn't have a girlfriend. She was really nice, though. She said she'd pose with me, if I wanted. So that's what we did. One of the waitresses took the picture."

Molly stared at the photo of Billy and Miss Delaney. Both of them looked younger, but not just in years. Molly remembered the last time she'd seen Miss Delaney and how very tired she had seemed.

"It probably sounds silly," Billy was saying. "But it meant a lot to me. Sometimes, when I was really scared and lonely, I pulled this picture out of my pocket and reminded myself that folks back in the States were pulling for me."

"That doesn't sound silly," Molly said quietly.

"I sent Darleen that rose pin as a thank-you,"

Billy said. "And you know, I always thought I'd look her up when I got back home. But now ... I don't think so. I'd rather just keep her this way, in the picture. She was a real doll. I could tell she had a soft heart. And she was a good listener, too."

*That's Miss Delaney*, Molly thought.

Billy began rubbing Bennett's ears. The dog gave a whimper of delight. "I hope Darleen didn't end up getting pestered because she was so nice," Billy added absently. "I heard later about this guy in another unit who'd sort of cracked, you know what I mean? He went overseas with a picture of him and a camera girl—who knows, it might have even been Darleen. At first, he told his pals that the girl in the picture was a camera girl. Then that guy got so lonely and scared that he came to believe that the camera girl was his *girlfriend*. Told everybody they were engaged, kept talking about the ring he was going to give her." Billy shook his head sadly. "Poor guy. I don't know what ever happened to him."

## AN UNEXPECTED VISITOR

Molly's heart slid toward her toes as she considered a troubling possibility. What if something similar had happened between Fletcher and Miss Delaney? Fletcher had used a common soldiers' phrase on the day he was arrested, so he might certainly be a veteran. And maybe he'd visited the Lucky Diamond before going overseas and had met Miss Delaney. Perhaps that's where all the trouble had started.

Molly got home that evening to an empty house. Mom was at a Red Cross meeting, Dad and Jill were at the hospital, Ricky was doing homework with a friend, and Mrs. Gilford had left a note saying that Mrs. Petroski was babysitting Brad. "I guess everyone thinks I'm mature enough to be on my own for a while," Molly grumbled as she helped herself to some leftover macaroni and cheese. She *wanted* her family to see her as mature. Still, it wasn't much fun to be home all by herself. ·

A little before seven o'clock that evening, Molly headed to Linda's house. When she saw Susan coming from the other direction, she waved her arm. "Boy-oh-boy," Molly said. "I've got all *kinds* of things to tell you."

When they reached the back steps, Molly heard a murmur of voices through the screened door. "Linda?" she called.

"Come on in."

Molly followed Susan into the kitchen. "I've figured part of it out!" Molly announced triumphantly. "You'll never guess..." Her voice died when she saw Linda's mother at the counter, energetically stirring something in a mixing bowl. She wore a ruffled yellow skirt, and her hair curled at her shoulders.

"Mrs. Rinaldi!" Molly exclaimed. "Aren't you going to work tonight?"

"All the women workers lost their jobs today," Mrs. Rinaldi said. "Suddenly I didn't know what to do with my time. So I'm making brownies! I've done so little baking lately that I had plenty of ration coupons for sugar."

# An Unexpected Visitor

Molly glanced at Linda, who raised her eyebrows and gave a little shrug.

"There's nothing to worry about," Mrs. Rinaldi added over her shoulder. "I took the job because I wanted to do my part for the war effort, not because we needed the paychecks."

"Everyone says the factory couldn't have made the planes without the women workers," Susan said.

Linda's mother looked out the window, and for a moment her hand stilled. "At first, I hated the work. It was noisy and dirty. And some of the men at the factory assumed that women couldn't work with machines and tools."

Molly thought about that. "You're reminding me of the way Ronnie Vanko told us we couldn't earn a medal because we were girls."

"And you're proving him wrong, I hope!" Mrs. Rinaldi began to pour batter into a waiting pan. "I came to love working at the factory. I did things I never dreamed I could do. And now— now everyone expects us to trade in our overalls for aprons and go back to baking pies. Some of the women don't have families. They're going to have a hard time adjusting. Thank goodness I have children at home to bake *for*." She smiled at the girls.

Molly thought that Mrs. Rinaldi's eyes looked sad, though. It seemed as if she wanted both things—to work *and* to be home. Would Mom feel that way when the war ended? Molly had just assumed that Mom would happily leave her job at the Red Cross when the war was finally won. But maybe it wouldn't be so simple for her, either.

Sometimes it seemed as if nothing would ever be simple again.

"These won't be ready for a while," Mrs. Rinaldi said, sliding the pan into the oven. "Linda, you may run along with your friends."

Once the girls were outside, Linda murmured, "Mom doesn't know what to do with all of her energy. Let's get out of here before she asks us to help dig a new flowerbed or something."

"We can go sit on my swing," Molly suggested.

Susan looked at the sky. "It looks like rain is

coming, but it might hold off for a while. Let's go."

When the girls reached the McIntires' swing, Molly dropped onto the seat and squeezed over to make room for her friends. "I have *got* to tell you something about Ronnie and Fletcher," she said eagerly. "And about Miss Delaney, too."

"What about Miss Delaney?" Susan said, her eyebrows rising.

Molly told them what she'd discovered at the veterans' hospital that afternoon. "So Miss Delaney worked as a camera girl at one of the nightclubs in town after the war began. She took photographs of soldiers with their wives and girlfriends, so the men would have nice mementos when they got to the front. But she posed *in* the picture with Billy."

Linda frowned. "Why? I don't get it."

"She was just being kind. I think she wanted to remind him that everyone at home, even strangers, were thinking about him. Billy said his picture was a real comfort."

"That would be just like Miss Delaney," Susan agreed.

"But Billy told me something else," Molly said. "He'd heard that after a camera girl posed with another soldier, that guy didn't understand that she was just being nice. Once he got to the war front, and got scared and lonely..." She spread her hands.

"He started to imagine that the camera girl really *was* his girlfriend?" Linda guessed.

"Exactly!" Molly said. "What if something like that had happened with—"

"Fletcher!" Susan gasped.

"I'm pretty sure he's a veteran," Molly said. "Maybe now that he's back, he wants to go out on a date with Miss Delaney."

Linda said quietly, "I'm glad my dad has a real family to send him pictures and letters."

"I know." Molly tried to imagine how lonely Dad had been in England. Had Dad made friends with the girl in his photo because his own children were so far away?

Susan's eyes were shining. "Maybe Fletcher fell madly in love with Miss Delaney," she said eagerly. "Just like in the movies!"

"But when she didn't return his affections, Fletcher got angry," Linda added.

Molly picked up the tale. "And now he's back in Jefferson, and he's still angry at her. That's why Miss Delaney seemed worried."

Susan sat up straighter as another idea struck. "Maybe *that's* why Miss Delaney didn't come to the veterans' hospital with us. Maybe she was afraid Fletcher would be there."

"Why would he be at the hospital?" Linda pushed her feet against the ground to get the swing started again. "We've seen him. He's not hurt."

"Not in a way we can *see*," Molly corrected. "But the soldiers with battle fatigue are wounded, too. Dad's helping to treat them. Maybe . . . well, if Fletcher *is* just back from the war, maybe he's being treated for battle fatigue."

"But why did Miss Delaney quit her volunteer job with the Red Cross so suddenly?" Linda demanded. "Why not even say good-bye to us?"

"I don't know," Molly admitted. "But listen! There's more news about Fletcher." She quickly told her friends about the fight at the factory.

"Gosh, Fletcher seems like a really bad guy," Susan said. She rubbed her arms as if she were chilled. "Poor Miss Delaney."

Linda tipped her head, considering. "We may be way off. If this Fletcher guy was making Miss Delaney nervous, why didn't she just go to the police?"

"The police had him once and let him go," Molly reminded them. "Officer Steves told me they're short-handed because so many officers enlisted—" Her voice broke when Susan clutched her arm in a painful grip. "*What?*" Molly demanded, trying to jerk her arm away.

Then she noticed that both of her friends were staring with wide eyes across the backyard. When Molly followed their gazes, her eyes went wide, too. A red-haired man in a plaid jacket had appeared from behind the garden shed and was striding toward them. His face was hard.

It was Fletcher.

# 11
## A NEW PLAN

The girls jumped to their feet and scrambled behind the swing. "Maybe we should run for it!" Susan whispered.

Molly was tempted by that idea, but refused to give in to it. After all, this was *her* yard! As Fletcher approached she yelled, "Go away!"

"Or we'll call the police!" Linda added.

Fletcher walked up to the swing. "Oh, *stop* it," he growled.

Molly didn't know what she had expected him to say, but that wasn't it. "You just—just get out of here!" she demanded.

"Not until we've had a talk."

"We don't have to talk to you!" Molly flared.

Linda said, "And if you hurt us—"

"I'm not going to hurt you!" he barked. "Do

you really think I'd hurt a bunch of kids?"

"We saw you get arrested for punching someone at the telephone company," Linda said.

"Yeah, and you picked a fight with that man at the factory for no reason," Molly added.

Fletcher's hands tensed into fists. Molly's skin grew clammy with sweat as she watched the tall man struggle with his temper. Maybe they *should* run. She wished desperately that Dad were home. *But he's not*, she thought. *It's up to me to make Fletcher go away.*

Maybe the best thing she could do was try to see what he wanted. "Okay," she managed, trying to keep her voice calm. "What do you want to talk about?"

"Ronnie," Fletcher said.

"R-Ronnie?" Susan squeaked.

"The poor kid's had a hard time," Fletcher said. "And you've been mean to him. I want you to knock it off." He ran a hand through his carrot-colored hair, looking nothing at all like a villain.

Molly exchanged confused glances with her

friends. "We haven't been mean to Ronnie," she began.

"Oh, yeah?" Fletcher took a step closer. Molly grabbed the swing to keep her hands from trembling. "That's not how I hear it," he said. "And on top of everything else, you just had to steal some of his paper, didn't you." His flat voice made the words a statement, not a question.

This was more confusing by the minute. "Steal his paper?" Molly echoed. "I never—"

"Don't lie!" he snapped.

Molly was getting tired of being accused of doing something she hadn't done. "I'm *not* lying!"

All of a sudden Fletcher looked more tired than angry. "Just give the poor kid a break," he said. "That's all I'm asking. Doesn't he have it rough enough already? How would you feel if *your* dad had been Missing in Action for so long?"

"*What?*" Molly gasped.

"Ronnie's dad is Missing in Action?" Linda asked. Susan's face had gone blank with surprise.

Fletcher's eyes narrowed. "Are you trying to tell me you didn't know?"

They shook their heads. "But that explains the coal," Molly said, almost to herself. Mom had told her that many families had a hard time financially if their soldier was declared Missing in Action. Molly was pretty sure that Ronnie had been scavenging for lumps of coal that fell from passing trains so that he and his mom would have fuel for their furnace.

Fletcher rubbed his face with his hands. "Oh, that kid," he mumbled.

"How do you even know Ronnie?" Molly asked.

"I'm his uncle. His mom is my sister."

"Oh-h-h." Molly finally understood why Ronnie had come to Fletcher's aid after the fight at the factory that morning. "And you said someone had stolen some paper from him? When?"

Fletcher reached into his pocket and pulled out a pack of cigarettes. Then he glanced at the girls, tucked the cigarettes back into his pocket, and pulled out a couple of peanuts instead.

"Well, sometime last night or today," he said, cracking one of the peanuts open. "Ronnie had a box of paper in the garage, and someone dumped it over."

"It wasn't me," Molly insisted. "It wasn't any of us. In fact . . . well, how do we know it wasn't *you*? Did you go into our garden shed and mess with *my* paper?" She felt her breathing quicken. Maybe it wasn't wise to push Fletcher like this, but she had to know. "It was you I saw in the yard that night, wasn't it? You'd been in the shed. It smelled like cigarette smoke. And I found a peanut shell in there."

Fletcher's face hardened again. He crushed another peanut shell and ate the nut before answering. "I *was* in your shed. I slept there a couple of times, and I spread a little paper out to help keep warm. That's all."

"But *why*?" Molly demanded. "If your sister lives right there—"

Fletcher sucked in a long breath of air and blew it out slowly. "I wanted to keep an eye on her and Ronnie," he said. "But at first, I didn't want them to know I was around. Not that it's any of your business."

He hadn't fully answered Molly's question. But the look in his eyes—a sadness so deep she felt her heart twist—kept her still.

"Look," Fletcher said. "You can think whatever you want about me. But give Ronnie a break." He started to turn away.

"Wait!" Molly cried.

"*Mol-ly*," Susan said in a low tone, the word squeezing between her teeth as if to say, *What are you doing? Let him go!*

Molly knew Susan was right, but it was too late to back down now. "What about Miss Delaney?" she said. "Are you making trouble for her? Did she quit her Red Cross job because—"

"Darleen Delaney," Fletcher growled, stabbing a finger toward the girls, "is my friend. No more, no less. She quit that job because she was exhausted. And your nosy questions were the last straw."

"They were?" Molly blinked back sudden hot tears. "But—but I just wanted to help her!"

# A New Plan

"Maybe so," Fletcher said. "But all you did was make her worry that our friendship was going to get me into even more trouble." With that, he turned away. The girls didn't move until Fletcher had crossed the backyard again and disappeared behind the lilac bushes toward Ronnie's house.

"Phew," Susan said. "I was scared out of my wits!"

Linda walked around the swing and dropped back onto it. "I don't get it," she said slowly. "If Fletcher is Ronnie's uncle, why did he want to sleep in your garden shed?"

"I think Fletcher is nuts," Susan said. "He can't go on sleeping in garden sheds and—and barging into people's backyards and frightening kids! We should call the police."

Molly exhaled slowly, loosening her cramped fingers from the back of the swing. If Fletcher had battle fatigue, he needed help more than he needed to be locked up. "No, let's wait to call the police," she said. "I'd like to talk to my dad about him. Okay?"

Linda nodded. Susan hesitated before saying, "Okay."

"What do you think about Fletcher saying Ronnie's dad is Missing in Action?" Linda asked. "It sounds like he's been missing for a long time."

"Well, it means Ronnie has been lying about his dad," Susan pointed out. "Or at least...not telling people the truth."

"It's horrible that Ronnie's dad is missing, though," Molly said. She remembered how much she had feared that Dad might get hurt or killed. To have him just disappear, to not know what had happened, would have been even worse.

"It *is* horrible. There's nothing we can do about it, though." Susan glanced up at the gathering clouds. "It's getting dark. I have to go home."

Molly was so deep in thought that it took her a moment to realize that Susan and Linda had both started away. "Hold on!" Molly cried. "We still have a mystery to solve! Fletcher may have been using my shed, but he's not the person who's been searching through everyone's stacks of waste paper."

Linda and Susan looked at each other. "I don't know if I can keep watch tonight," Linda said. "Not with my mother home."

"But tonight is probably the last chance we have!" Molly protested. "We're supposed to deliver our first batch of paper to the Red Cross tomorrow! Whoever is searching for something— a counterfeiter, or a spy, or whoever—will know he only has tonight to find whatever he lost."

Susan shivered again. "I think I've had enough adventures for one day. Besides, it's probably going to rain. I'm sorry, Molly. It looks like you're on your own."

Molly didn't know what to do about the Paper Prowler. She decided that she did have something important to take care of first, though. A few minutes later, she took a deep breath and knocked on the Vankos' front door. When it opened and she saw Ronnie standing there, she didn't know if she was glad or sorry that he was home.

"What do *you* want?" Ronnie demanded.

Molly rubbed her palms on her skirt. "I—um—well, I just wanted to say that I heard about your dad. Being missing, I mean. And I'm sorry—"

Ronnie threw a quick look over his shoulder, then glared at Molly. "You just shut your stupid mouth," he hissed. "You don't know *anything!*" Then he slammed the door in her face.

Molly quickly walked back down the steps and began to cut through the Vankos' yard. Well, she'd tried. She didn't know what else to do.

She increased her pace when she heard the Vankos' back door open and shut behind her, afraid that Ronnie had decided to hurl more insults at her. "Hey," a low voice called.

Molly whirled and saw Fletcher. "I was just trying to apologize," she began.

He waved her to silence. "I know. I was inside, and I heard you. Thanks for that."

"You're welcome. Ronnie's still mad at me, though."

"He'll come around." Fletcher rubbed his neck. "He envies you, you know. Can you imagine how he feels when he sees you and your dad together?"

Molly remembered Ronnie watching her and Dad talking and hugging. She'd thought Ronnie was spying on her! But instead . . .

"And, listen," Fletcher added. "I'm sorry if I scared you girls earlier. Ronnie was upset about his paper, and he was *sure* you were responsible. I just wanted to talk to you."

Molly wasn't sure what to say. She'd seen Fletcher get arrested for punching someone. She'd seen Fletcher start an argument that turned into a fight. She still didn't know exactly what had happened between this young man and Miss Delaney. But right now, Fletcher just seemed like a worried uncle.

And it occurred to her that maybe, just maybe, he could help Ronnie and help *her* at the same time.

"I didn't know for sure that Ronnie was collecting scrap paper," she said. Feeling the first sprinkles of rain, she zipped up her jacket.

Several emotions chased across Fletcher's face: grief, shame, anger, perhaps something else. "He's trying, but he hasn't collected much," Fletcher said. "No time. Ronnie wanted to help out his mom, so he got a job delivering groceries."

*That's probably what Ronnie was doing with his wagon,* Molly thought. And why Ronnie didn't have time to help with war efforts. Why he didn't always get his homework done. Why he was too tired to play at recess.

"I wish he'd told us about his dad," she told Fletcher. "Maybe we could have helped him."

Fletcher shook his head. "Ronnie's mom won't admit that her husband might not be coming back," he said, sounding weary. "She told Ronnie not to discuss it. It's like she thinks that everything will be all right as long as she *acts* like it is. I'm trying to help her realize that pretending isn't doing Ronnie any good, but

I haven't convinced her yet."

Molly thought about all the times that she and Ronnie had clashed. She wished she could do some things over. No wonder he'd talked so much about his dad's heroic deeds! Those stories were all he had left of his father.

"I'm really, really sorry," she told Fletcher. "But it wasn't me—or any of us kids—who messed up his paper. Honest! In fact, all of us around here are having the same problem. I think someone is trying to find some papers that got collected by mistake. Maybe a counterfeiter. Maybe a spy. I don't know! But tomorrow is the first collection date, so if the guy is going to be caught, it has to be tonight."

Fletcher frowned with confusion. "I don't understand."

"I don't understand everything either," Molly admitted. "But I have a plan. I can't do it by myself, though. So . . . well, would you be willing to help?"

## Clues in the Shadows

Later that night, after Mom and Dad had gone to bed, Molly and Ricky crept down the stairs. Twilight's sprinkle had given way to a steady rain, so they silently pulled on their raincoats and boots. "Stay," Molly whispered to Bennett when the dog came to investigate.

When Ricky and Molly got outside, they paused on the back steps. "You're sure this Fletcher guy is back there?" Ricky asked.

Molly squinted, trying to peer through the streaming darkness. Yes, near the shed—two quick flashes of light. She answered the signal with two flashes from her own light. "He's there," she said. "Do you have the other flashlights?"

"Right here," Ricky assured her. "Okay. I'll be over by the garage." In an instant he was gone. Molly tugged at the hood on her raincoat and settled down on the back steps to wait.

*Maybe no one will come*, she thought some time later. She was cold. She was tired. And despite her best efforts, she was getting wet. Even huddled against the wall, with her hood pulled down as far as it would go, her glasses were streaked with water. If the Paper Prowler did show up, she wasn't sure she'd even be able to see him.

But she wouldn't admit defeat. Fletcher, hiding in the lilac bushes, was surely even wetter than she was. Ricky hadn't given up, either.

Once she'd told Ricky everything, he'd been enthusiastic about helping. "Yeah!" he'd said, smacking one fist into his palm. "We can set a trap!"

Molly had nodded. "Right. I tried keeping watch by myself, but the Paper Prowler didn't come. If I watched by myself tonight and I *did* see the prowler, all I'd be able to do is scare him off. Or maybe get a good look, so I could describe him to the police. But Mr. Fletcher was a soldier. He helped me come up with a good plan. He figured that if the Paper Prowler shows up, you could shine flashlights on him. Then Mr. Fletcher will tackle him and hold onto him while I run inside and call the police."

Molly still thought it was a good plan. It

wouldn't have been safe for her to try and confront a crook or criminal by herself. Mom wouldn't have helped her, and she couldn't ask Dad, either. This way, if no one did come, Mom and Dad would never be the wiser. And if she and Ricky *did* help catch some crook or criminal . . . well, Molly figured her parents would be understanding. Maybe even proud.

She just hoped the Paper Prowler would show up *soon*.

Another hour or so crept past. Despite her discomfort, Molly was fighting sleepiness when she suddenly became aware of—of *something*. She jerked upright, instantly alert. She didn't hear anything but the endless rain, pounding the roof and gushing from the downspout and thudding against the softened earth. And she couldn't see anything but streaming blackness.

Quivering with excitement, Molly waited for whatever had caught her attention. There—a tiny flash of light, quickly extinguished. After a moment it came again. She squinted through her rain-streaked glasses. It looked as if someone was creeping across the backyard, turning a flashlight on from time to time as if to check his path, then quickly turning it back off.

Was Ricky still awake? Was Fletcher watching? Molly stifled the urge to shout a warning. *They* would move first. The whole plan depended on her staying silent and still until they did.

Another quick flash—farther away now. Almost to the garden shed. Molly's muscles tensed, ready to spring into action.

"*Yah!*" Ricky bellowed. Two beams of light cut through the rain. The intruder froze in the sudden glare. Then another shadowy figure appeared as Fletcher launched himself from his hiding place. He was in the air as he appeared in the twin beams of light. But instead of landing on the prowler, he twisted at the last moment and did a wild somersault onto the ground.

Molly ran toward the shed, her feet slipping on the muddy ground. She and Ricky reached the shed as Fletcher scrambled to his feet. "Don't let the prowler get away!" Molly gasped. "Grab him!"

The prowler, though, wasn't moving. Molly squinted through her glasses. Then her shoulders sagged. "Oh, no," she moaned. "Mrs. Petroski? Is that you? *Again?*"

Mrs. Petroski was almost hidden in a big raincoat that had probably belonged to her husband. She pushed the hood back with a shaking hand.

Molly wanted to cry. All of this effort—for nothing! If the real Paper Prowler had been nearby, he was long gone now. She blew out a long, disappointed breath. "I'm sorry we frightened you, Mrs. Petroski. Is Marmalade gone again?"

"Marmalade was never gone," Mrs. Petroski said. She hung her head. "And I can't keep lying. I'm the guilty one, Molly. Go ahead and call the police."

# 12
## SECRETS

"What?" Molly gasped. "Call the police? *Why?*"

Before the elderly woman could answer, the back door banged open and the outside light flared on. "Who's there?" Dad called sternly. "What's going on out there?"

"Maybe we should all go inside and sort this out," Fletcher said. He took Mrs. Petroski's arm and led the way.

Molly and Ricky trailed along behind. "Great work, Molly," Ricky muttered. "All you caught was our next-door neighbor!"

"But why did she tell us to call the police?"

"She's afraid we're going to arrest her for trespassing!" Ricky hissed. "And now Dad's up, too! Mom's going to be furious." He bumped her with his shoulder.

"It's not *my* fault," Molly protested, bumping him back. "You agreed!"

"But it was your stupid plan!" He bumped her harder.

Molly's feet slipped from under her. She landed with a thud and a splash in a cold, muddy corner of their Victory garden. But as she fell, she grabbed Ricky's ankle and pulled. He landed right beside her.

Molly's glasses were splattered with mud now. When she took them off she saw Dad's feet, still in their slippers, appear right beside her. "Molly?" he asked. "Ricky? What on *earth* is going on?"

Molly exchanged a guilty glance with her brother as they struggled to their feet. In the outside light's yellow glow, she could see that Ricky was mud-smeared, head to toe—just as she was.

Dad stood in the pouring rain, his pajamas and robe plastered to his skin. He suddenly made a strange snuffling noise. *Oh no*, Molly thought. On top of everything else, they'd upset Dad.

Then the snuffling noises grew into something larger. Something she hadn't heard in a long, long time. Molly's heart grew light. Dad wasn't upset after all—Dad was laughing!

Twenty minutes later, everyone was sitting around the kitchen table. Mom had made a big pot of tea. Molly, Dad, and Ricky had changed into dry clothes. Mrs. Petroski's big raincoat and boots had kept her dry. Fletcher had wiped his face and shrugged into a wool shirt of Dad's, saying that was all he needed.

"Okay," Dad said. "What is this all about?"

Molly quickly explained everything that had led up to this night's excitement. "And then I recognized Mrs. Petroski," she concluded.

"I recognized her too," Fletcher added. "I managed to twist away just in time!"

Everyone looked at their elderly neighbor. "I've been trying to find something," Mrs. Petroski quavered. "Something I lost."

"What did you lose?" Molly asked.

"A letter from my brother," Mrs. Petroski said. "It must have gotten mixed in with some scrap paper by mistake. I knew one of the neighborhood children had collected it, but I didn't know who! So I've been trying to find it. I'd already looked through the paper in your garage, but Brad mentioned that there was more in your garden shed."

"But if you'd only told us what you'd lost, we could have helped you look!" Molly said. "We thought the Paper Prowler was a counterfeiter or a German spy! Someone bad."

Mrs. Petroski stared at her teacup. "My brother is not a German spy," she said. "But he *is* a German soldier. He's in a prison camp."

Molly blinked at her. Sweet Mrs. Petroski had a brother fighting for America's enemy?

"I was born in Germany," she told them. "My brother was just a baby when I left for America, many years ago. I had studied English and spoke it well. I soon met and married my husband, and we moved to Jefferson. Everyone assumed I had a Polish background, as he did. I heard people say horrible things about Germans, so I never told anyone where I was born. And then, when this world war started . . ." She gave them a pleading look. "What could I do?"

Molly knew that many Americans hated all German people. And when Dad was in danger of being bombed, or when she read about some of the terrible things the German government had done, Molly sometimes felt the same way.

"I didn't even know my brother was in the army," Mrs. Petroski went on. "Then a few weeks ago, I got a letter from him. I was glad to learn that he's all right! But I was also terrified that someone might find out that my brother is a German prisoner of war. *That's* why I was trying so hard to find my letter."

The look on the widow's face made Molly ache inside.

"I understand if you want to call the police," Mrs. Petroski said.

"Of course we won't call the police!" Molly blurted. Dad shook his head as well.

A tear rolled down one of Mrs. Petroski's wrinkled cheeks. "Thank you for that," she said. "I am a proud American citizen. I'm ashamed of the horrible things that some German people have done. But not all German people are evil."

"No, of course not," Mom said quietly. "And the Red Cross can help you stay in touch with your brother, without anyone else being the wiser. Right now, though, I think everyone needs to get some sleep."

"I'll walk Mrs. Petroski home," Ricky offered.

After Ricky and the neighbor left, Mom said good night and disappeared upstairs. "Mr. Fletcher," Molly said, and then hesitated. "I don't mean to pry, but... well, for starters, why do you keep getting into fights?"

Fletcher looked at Dad. "You think I should try to talk about it?"

Dad spread his hands. "That's up to you."

Molly stared from one man to the other. *So Fletcher knows Dad*, she thought. It sounded like Fletcher *was* struggling with battle fatigue.

Fletcher leaned against the counter. "Before

the war, I worked for the telephone company. I did a good job, too. When I came back from the front, I went to see about getting my old job back. But somebody had told my boss that I was being treated for battle fatigue. Because of that, he refused to hire me again."

"But—but that's not fair!" Molly said.

"I told him I'd be fine working as a lineman," Fletcher said. "By myself, outside. He still said no. And I stood there, looking around at all the shirkers who had never gone to fight for our country, and they still all had their jobs, and—" He gave a small, exhausted shrug. "And I lost my temper. Next thing I knew, I'd decked the guy. Fortunately, he decided not to press charges, so the police let me go."

Molly knew that punching someone was never a good idea. But she understood why Fletcher had gotten angry.

"And that time at the factory gate?" Fletcher continued. "I was waiting for my sister to get off shift. And I hear this guy beside me say, 'My wife's making so much money, I hope the war goes on forever!' And I thought about all I went through over in Europe, and my dead buddies, and about Ronnie's dad, and—and I just couldn't stand there and listen to that guy gloat about getting rich."

"Oh," Molly said in a small voice. "I'm sorry I told the guard to call the police."

"That's okay," Fletcher said. He turned toward the door. "I'll see you around, kid."

"Do you need a place to stay tonight?" Dad asked.

The tall man shook his head. "No, thanks. I've been staying at my sister's house. You were right when you said she'd want me there."

"Thanks for your help," Molly called after him. She realized that she *still* didn't know why Miss Delaney had seemed to be afraid of him on Victory in Europe day, since he'd said they were friends. But Molly had learned enough to know that the situation might not be what it seemed.

When Fletcher had gone, Dad said, "Well, Molly. You've had quite a night."

"Dad? You met Mr. Fletcher at the veterans' hospital, right?"

"That's right," Dad said.

"Why didn't Mr. Fletcher just move in with his sister when he got home?"

Dad scratched his chin thoughtfully. "I can't discuss the details of his case, but I think it's okay to say that he was afraid people would tease Ronnie if they knew his uncle had been sent home with battle fatigue. And I think he's a little ashamed that he hasn't been able to find work. He didn't want to be a burden."

"It's not fair," Molly said again.

Dad took off his glasses and rubbed his eyes. "No, it's not. But most people simply don't understand what war can do to a person."

"I didn't," Molly admitted. "It didn't occur to me at first that Mr. Fletcher might be sick."

"Battle fatigue affects every soldier differently," Dad told her. "Some get nightmares. Some try to hide from their memories by drinking alcohol. Some develop a temper, like Mr. Fletcher."

"I'm glad soldiers with battle fatigue have you to help them," Molly said.

"Other than listening, I'm not much good at helping them." Dad twiddled his teaspoon between his fingers. "I don't have the specialized training for that. I've learned what little I know about battle fatigue by attending meetings for soldiers who are struggling with it."

"You went to those meetings so you could learn how to treat the men?"

"No, Molly." Dad put the teaspoon down and looked her in the eye. "I went so that I could get help, too. I have my own bad memories. Most of the time I'm fine! But sometimes, when I think about the bad times, my hands begin to shake. That's why I started knitting—to keep them busy."

Molly remembered how Fletcher had fumbled with his cigarette pack and how he often cracked peanut shells. He probably needed to keep his hands busy, too.

"I'm proud of you for serving our country, Dad," Molly told him. "But I'm also sorry that you had such terrible times."

"I tried to prepare myself," Dad said slowly. "I knew I'd be treating badly wounded soldiers. But I hadn't realized that I'd be treating so many civilians, too. There was this little girl, Jeannie— she used to come by the doctors' quarters. Her own father was off at war. She was visiting one day when a bomb fell near the hospital. She got cut in the arm by a piece of flying glass. As I stitched up the wound, I felt like my heart was breaking. She reminded me so much of *you*."

"Oh, Dad." Molly ran around the table and put her head on his shoulder. He wrapped his arms around her. For a long moment they didn't move. The only sound was the rain on the roof.

Finally Molly pulled away. "Dad? Thanks for telling me about Jeannie. I thought you wouldn't tell me things because you didn't realize how much I'd grown up."

Dad shook his head. "Sometimes veterans can only talk to other veterans. It doesn't mean that they don't love their children. They just feel most comfortable talking to people who know firsthand what they've been through."

Molly nodded. That did make sense.

"And how can you think I don't know how much you've grown up?" Dad went on. "I can see it! Sometimes it makes me sad. It reminds me of all the time I missed. I left a house full of noisy kids who argued and teased and got into mischief. I came home to something very different."

"We thought you needed peace and quiet!" Molly exclaimed. "You'll never know how hard it's been to be good!"

They stared at each other. Then both of them burst out laughing. "Well, gosh and golly, olly Molly," Dad managed. "I sure am glad to hear that." And they started laughing all over again.

*It'll take more time,* Molly thought. More time for Dad to get used to being home. But she was pretty sure that her family, at least, was going to be all right.

# EPILOGUE

Molly ran down the corridor to the big room used for school assemblies. When she opened the door, she was relieved to see that the program had not yet started.

Almost two months had passed since she'd found Mrs. Petroski hunting for her brother's letter. School had ended. The air had turned sticky-hot. Still, a good crowd had turned out for the special Red Cross reception. Molly was pleased to see so many of her friends and neighbors.

Linda and Susan darted through the gathering to join her. "We thought you weren't going to make it!" Susan said.

"I was at the veterans' hospital with Bennett," Molly explained breathlessly. "Dad says Bennett does as much good as the doctors!" She'd been taking Bennett to the hospital several times a week. Sometimes Dad took Bennett along when the men with combat fatigue got together, too.

"We saw your parents," Susan added. "They brought Mrs. Petroski."

"Good," Molly said. Mrs. Petroski's letter had never been found. Molly hadn't told her friends about Mrs. Petroski's brother, but that was one secret she was happy to keep.

Then she stood on tiptoe, craning her neck. "Look! Miss Delaney's here!" Molly waved her arm wildly.

When Miss Delaney spotted the girls, she slid through the crowd to join them. "Oh, it's so good to see you!" she said.

Molly studied her friend anxiously. She hadn't seen Miss Delaney since their conversation at the Red Cross building all those weeks ago, and she'd been worried about her. Now Molly was relieved to see that Miss Delaney looked . . . well, healthier somehow. Happier, perhaps, and certainly more rested.

"Are you feeling better?" Susan asked.

"Yes," Miss Delaney said simply. "I couldn't possibly miss this ceremony. And I wanted to see some of my favorite JRC girls." She spread her arms in that familiar gesture, making sure each of them knew that they were included. Molly felt warm inside.

"And I wanted to explain about Tommy, too," Miss Delaney added. "Mr. Fletcher, I mean. He told me that you'd had a little talk."

"That's right," Molly said, "but there are some things I still don't understand. Did you meet him when you worked as a camera girl?"

"I did," Miss Delaney said. "And we struck up a true friendship. We wrote to each other the whole time he was gone. When he came back, and I saw how much anger had built up inside him ... well, I was worried sick. I was frightened on Victory in Europe day, Molly, but not *of* him. *For* him. I was afraid that all the sudden noise and crush of people would upset him."

Molly nodded, remembering. It would have been horrible if something had made

Mr. Fletcher lose his temper on that special day.

"And I couldn't explain that to you," Miss Delaney said, "because I didn't have his permission to discuss his condition. When you tried to talk to me that afternoon at the Red Cross building, I suddenly felt as if my friendship might be doing Tommy Fletcher more harm than good. And I just thought, *I can't do this anymore.*"

Molly thought that over. Since the war had started, she'd had one or two moments like that, too.

Miss Delaney studied her fingers. "That's why I resigned from my Red Cross duties so suddenly. I was afraid I'd get sick myself if I didn't take a little break."

"What have you been doing?" Linda asked.

Miss Delaney's face brightened. "I'm working in the photography studio again. I lost my job at the airplane factory, just as your mother did. I was proud to do my part, but I must say, I never liked the work. I love being back in the photo studio." She paused as a thumping noise overpowered the hum of conversation.

Mrs. Gallagher was tapping a microphone. "That's my cue!" Miss Delaney said.

"We'd better grab seats!" Molly said. She didn't want to miss a minute of the ceremony.

The three girls slid into chairs near the front. Molly caught a glimpse of Mr. Fletcher farther down the row with his sister and Ronnie. Molly almost didn't recognize Ronnie wearing a shirt and tie and with his hair slicked back. *It's good to see them all here*, Molly thought. Mr. Fletcher hadn't found a job yet, but he'd finally accepted the fact that his sister and nephew were proud of his service and glad to have him home. And in Miss Delaney, Fletcher had at least one good friend to turn to.

Miss Delaney climbed the steps to the stage and walked to the microphone. "Thank you all for coming," she said. "It's time to reveal the results of our Paper Trooper Campaign! Our students worked very hard. Eighteen children earned Paper Trooper Certificates of Merit."

Molly glanced anxiously at her friends as Miss Delaney began to read the names, one by one. It was hard not to bounce with impatience as the beaming children went up onstage to collect their certificates from Mrs. Gallagher.

"The suspense is really getting to me!" Susan whispered. "I don't think I'll be able to stand it if—"

"Don't say it!" Molly hissed. "You'll jinx it!"

There was a long pause as the certificate winners posed for a group photograph. "Oh, come *on!*" Linda moaned in a low voice. "Get on with it!"

When the Certificate of Merit winners had finally left the stage, Miss Delaney addressed the crowd again. "And I'm proud to announce that one of our students managed to earn the top honor," she continued. "An Eisenhower medal."

Susan squirmed with excitement. "Do you think we collected enough?" she whispered.

"I sure hope so," Molly whispered back. Linda held up her hands, showing crossed fingers.

Miss Delaney said, "And the winner is . . . Ronnie Vanko!"

# Epilogue

Molly exchanged a triumphant smile with her two best friends. After learning how hard Ronnie had been working to help his family, the girls had organized an army of young Paper Prowlers. Each day while Ronnie was out delivering groceries, his classmates had crept into the Vankos' garage and deposited onto his pile whatever paper they'd collected. Dr. McIntire, who had offered to drive Ronnie and his paper to the weighing station each week, reported that Ronnie had been bewildered by the unexpected donations, but grateful.

Now, Ronnie was staring at Miss Delaney with wide eyes. Molly saw Mrs. Vanko and Mr. Fletcher urging Ronnie to his feet. Finally Ronnie stood, wiped his palms on his trousers, and slowly climbed to the stage. Mrs. Gallagher held a small open box. Miss Delaney took the Eisenhower medal from the box and carefully pinned it on Ronnie's shirt. The gold disk glimmered in the stage light. Ronnie's face glowed just as brightly.

After the local newspaper photographer had

his shots, Miss Delaney thanked everyone for coming and urged them to enjoy the refreshments waiting on tables in the back. "Let's go get some punch!" Linda exclaimed.

"You two go ahead," Molly said. "I'll find you in a few minutes."

She approached the Vankos just as Ronnie's mother put an arm around his shoulders. "Your father would be so proud!" Mrs. Vanko was saying. "We can display your Eisenhower medal right beside your dad's Distinguished Flying Cross."

Molly wanted to speak to Ronnie but more people pressed around, giving him handshakes and claps on the back. She watched as Alison Hargate and her mother congratulated Ronnie. Alison beamed, and her mother even managed a smile. "Thank you," Ronnie said politely. He rubbed the medal pinned on his shirt as if wanting to remind himself that it was real.

Then he caught Molly's eye. He pointed at the Eisenhower medal and then at her, with a question in his eyes: *Are you responsible for this?*

Molly shrugged and gestured broadly at the crowd: *You have lots of friends in Jefferson*. He nodded, then gave her a thumbs-up sign.

Mom and Dad joined Molly. "Gosh and golly, olly Molly," Dad said. "Watching Ronnie win that medal was terrific. You kids surely did the most wonderful thing in the history of paper drives."

Molly accepted Dad's hug gratefully. He was sounding more like his old self every day. "A medal can't make up for Ronnie's dad being missing," she said. "But maybe it will help a little to know that people cared enough to want to help him."

Mom squeezed her shoulder. "I'm sure it will. We're very proud of you."

"Mom? Dad?" Molly looked up at her parents. "Wars don't really end when the shooting stops, do they."

"I'm afraid not," Dad said. "We've got a lot of challenges ahead of us at the veterans' hospital."

"And the Red Cross is already looking for

new ways to help returning soldiers and their families," Mom added.

Dad put an arm around Molly's shoulders. "We'll need your help."

"Good," Molly said. "I'm ready to go."

YOUR SCRAP
...brought it down
KEEP
SCRAPPING
IRON AND STEEL—RUBBER
ALL OTHER METALS—RAGS
MOVE ALL SCRAP NOW!

# LOOKING BACK

# A PEEK INTO THE PAST

As soon as the United States entered World War Two in December 1941, the government asked every American—grown-ups and kids alike—to pitch in and help win the war. Tens of millions of children became volunteers in the nation's massive war effort.

Children's wartime activities were often organized as competitions. Schools, classrooms, or individual kids vied to sell the most war bonds, collect the most scrap metal or waste paper, knit the most blankets, or roll the most bandages.

By the time Molly's mystery takes place, America had been at war for more than three years. Children still tried hard to be patriotic, but many were growing tired because of constant worry about the war and the pressure to take part in endless drives and campaigns. Adults were concerned about the toll the war effort was taking on children, but the nation's needs were so great that the campaigns continued.

In 1945, the military needed paper so desperately that General Dwight Eisenhower himself sponsored a national paper drive. As the leader

*The Eisenhower medal*

of American troops in Europe, Eisenhower was a national hero. The Eisenhower medal described in the story was actually awarded only to Boy Scouts, but a similar competition, called the Double V Paper Salvage Drive,

*Armfuls of scrap paper*

was launched in schools across the country at the same time, and it awarded medals and certificates, too.

The victory in Europe on May 8, 1945 (VE Day), sparked tremendous celebration and offered hope that the war in the Pacific might soon be over, too. But as more and

*Crowds cheer at the news of victory.*

more soldiers came home, they and their families faced new challenges. After years apart, both soldiers and their families had changed, and they had to get to know one another again. And nearly all veterans found it hard to talk about their experiences with relatives and friends who had never seen war firsthand.

*An English child hugs an American soldier on VE Day.*

Many soldiers who had lived through terrible experiences suffered from what people in Molly's time called "combat fatigue" or "battle jitters." Today this condition is known as *post-traumatic stress disorder,* or PTSD. Doctors tried to help these soldiers, but treatments weren't yet well developed. And in the 1940s, many Americans were fearful of people who received psychological treatment. Because of this, many troubled soldiers didn't seek help—and some who did were ridiculed and even denied jobs.

*Dogs sometimes provided comfort and companionship to soldiers.*

Thousands of soldiers never returned from the war. More than 180,000 American children lost their fathers in World War Two. Although it may be hard to imagine today, these families often kept their situation hidden because they felt ashamed or embarrassed by other people's pity. Families of soldiers listed as MIA, or

Missing in Action (meaning that no one knew whether the soldier was alive or dead) struggled with especially confusing emotions, as well as real financial hardship. Some children had to take on family responsibilities far beyond their years.

Despite the hardships, women on the home front did their best to support the troops. As men headed off to war, young women who volunteered for organizations such as the Red Cross tried hard to give the soldiers something happy to remember, even if it was just an evening of dancing or an hour of conversation. "Camera girls" like the fictional Darleen Delaney took photos of parting couples and sometimes

posed with a lonely soldier to give him a keepsake of home.

Nearly two million American women took jobs to help the war effort, as Linda's mother did. Others, like Molly's mother, handled challenging volunteer positions. By the spring of 1945, however, women were being urged to give up their factory jobs or were even laid off so that returning soldiers could find work.

Some women were happy to become homemakers again, but others never forgot the pride they felt in their wartime work. Through their example and encouragement, these women showed girls like Molly that they could be anything they wanted to be when they grew up.

*A poster urging American women to take jobs during the war*

# ABOUT THE AUTHOR

Kathleen Ernst grew up in Maryland in a house full of books. She wrote her first historical novel when she was fifteen and has been hooked ever since!

Today she and her husband live in Wisconsin. Her books for children and teens include *Secrets in the Hills: A Josefina Mystery* and two Kit mysteries, *Danger at the Zoo* and *Midnight in Lonesome Hollow*. She also wrote three American Girl History Mysteries: *Trouble at Fort La Pointe*, *Whistler in the Dark*, and *Betrayal at Cross Creek*.

*Trouble at Fort La Pointe* was an Edgar Allan Poe Award nominee for Best Children's Mystery. *Danger at the Zoo, Whistler in the Dark*, and *Betrayal at Cross Creek* were all nominated for the Agatha Award for Best Children's/Young Adult Mystery.